"We meet again."

As he parroted her words from Sunday back to her, she came to an abrupt halt.

Fletch gestured toward the overstuffed tote bags. "You look like you could use a hand. Where are you parked?"

Rachel finally looked up—and his breath jammed in his lungs.

Her jade eyes shimmered, and when she swallowed and moistened her lips, a twinge of some unidentifiable emotion tugged at his heart.

He cleared his throat—and softened his tone. "Your car?"

Rachel gestured to her right. "The silver Focus." As she led the way soft wisps of hair that had escaped her braid whispered at the neck of her sleeveless knit top, calling out to be touched.

While she popped the trunk with the remote, he took a deep breath.

Don't go there, Fletcher. Rachel Shaw might be attractive, but you don't need a summertime romance. She's the niece of your grandmother's best friend. This would only complicate your life.

Books by Irene Hannon

Love Inspired

*Home for the Holidays
*A Groom of Her Own
*A Family to Call Her Own
 It Had to Be You
 One Special Christmas
 The Way Home
 Never Say Goodbye
 Crossroads
†The Best Gift
†Gift from the Heart
†The Unexpected Gift
 All Our Tomorrows
 The Family Man
 Rainbow's End
**From This Day Forward
**A Dream to Share

**Where Love Abides
 Apprentice Father
††Tides of Hope
††The Hero Next Door
††The Doctor's Perfect Match
††A Father for Zach
 Child of Grace
§Seaside Reunion
§Finding Home
§Seaside Blessings
 Second Chance Summer

*Vows
†Sisters & Brides
**Heartland Homecoming
††Lighthouse Lane
§Starfish Bay

IRENE HANNON,

who writes both romance and romantic suspense, is the author of more than forty novels. Her books have been honored with two coveted RITA® Awards, a National Readers' Choice Award, a Carol Award, two HOLT Medallions, a Retailers Choice Award, a Daphne du Maurier Award and two Reviewers' Choice Awards from *RT Book Reviews* magazine. In addition, she is a Christy Award finalist, and *Booklist* named one of her novels a "Top 10 Inspirational Fiction" title for 2011. A former corporate communications executive with a Fortune 500 company, Irene now writes full-time from her home in Missouri. For more information, visit www.irenehannon.com.

Second Chance Summer
Irene Hannon

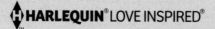
HARLEQUIN® LOVE INSPIRED®

Recycling programs for this product may not exist in your area.

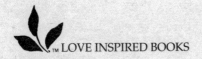

™ LOVE INSPIRED BOOKS

ISBN-13: 978-0-373-81770-2

SECOND CHANCE SUMMER

Copyright © 2014 by Irene Hannon

www.Harlequin.com

Printed in U.S.A.

Many are the plans of the human heart,
but it is the decision of the Lord that endures.
—*Proverbs* 19:21

To the Hannon clan—
Mom & Dad
Jim, Teresa, Catherine & Maureen
My husband, Tom (an honorary Hannon!)

And to Jekyll…our special island

Thanks for the memories.

Chapter One

Man, could that guy swim.

Under cover of her wide-brimmed hat and sunglasses, Rachel Shaw kept a discreet eye on the powerful shoulders cutting through the water a hundred feet beyond the crashing surf. The swimmer was moving as fast and effortlessly as the ubiquitous Jekyll Island dolphins that had been cavorting in almost that same spot yesterday.

And he'd been at it since before she'd arrived on the beach twenty minutes ago. Yet other than the few brief times he'd floated on his back while switching strokes, he showed no sign of tiring or slowing down.

Impressive.

A soft, snuffling sigh sounded close to her ear, and she looked over at the golden retriever flopped down next to her low-slung beach chair. He, too, was watching the figure in the water—until he turned to her with a pleading "Can we please swim, too?" look.

"Sorry, boy." She patted his head. "I promised Aunt Eleanor I wouldn't bring you home sopping wet. But we'll play a quick game of Frisbee in a few minutes."

At the word *Frisbee,* his ears perked up and his tail began to sweep the sand.

"I thought you'd like that. But give me five more minutes to veg."

Leaning back in her chair, Rachel tossed her book into her tote bag, abandoning any pretense of reading. It wasn't every day a woman got treated to such a demonstration of athletic prowess. And a quick scan left and right confirmed she had the show all to herself. Ah, deserted beaches—one of the beauties of summering on an off-the-beaten-path barrier island in Georgia.

Well, not quite deserted.

Her gaze swung back to the man in the water—who suddenly changed direction and headed for shore.

As Rachel followed his progress, her canine companion put his chin on her knee.

"Getting anxious, are we?" She gave him a distracted pat, her focus still on the dark-haired swimmer as she waited for him to stride from the sea like some mighty Greek god, all muscles and brawn and sinew.

Didn't happen.

Instead, he washed up on shore like a limp piece

of seaweed, then scuttled backward with his hands, away from the frothy surf.

Sheesh.

Talk about a letdown.

Adjusting her glasses, Rachel watched him fiddle with his ankle as he sat at the waterline. Maybe he'd had a close encounter with one of the jellyfish that were sometimes a painful nuisance here.

At the soft whimper beside her, she tugged the Frisbee out of her tote bag. Whatever was going on with that guy, he seemed well able to take care of himself.

"Okay, boy. You've been patient. Time for a quick game."

After settling her hat more firmly on her head, she stood and moved away from her chair. Throwing against the stiff breeze would be nuts; better to face the swimmer and aim the Frisbee his direction.

As she made the first toss, the man rose to his feet, diverting her attention.

Squinting into the sun, she peered at his left knee. Was that an elastic bandage?

Even as the question echoed in her mind, he sent her a quick look, picked up the towel that was draped over his duffel bag…and turned his back without the merest hint of appreciative interest.

Huh.

That wasn't the usual male response when she wore her swimsuit.

At the unexpected twinge of disappointment, Rachel huffed out a breath, straightened her shoulders and smoothed a hand over her hip. She might not be eighteen anymore, but her thirty-three-year-old body had held up fine.

Besides, why should she care whether a stranger noticed her? It wasn't as if romance was on her agenda for this visit. Her goals were the same this year as they'd been for the past three summers: rest, recharge and renew. And a broad-shouldered guy who swam like a fish wasn't going to change that—no matter how good-looking he might be.

She took the Frisbee from her eager companion and tossed it again, doing her best to give the other occupant of the beach the same I-couldn't-care-less treatment he was giving her.

Except a gust of wind snatched the Frisbee and hurled it straight toward the man's back as he pulled a T-shirt over his head—and her canine friend, in hot pursuit, was focused only on the soaring blue plastic disk.

Uh-oh.

"Hey!" Rachel jogged forward, waving her arms. As the distance between man and dog shrank at a frightening pace, her pulse tripped into fast forward and she doubled her volume. "Hey, mister!"

Just as the man turned, seventy pounds of golden fur took flight toward the broad chest.

Rachel came to an abrupt halt, cringed and closed her eyes.

Five seconds ticked by before she had the courage to peek at the scene.

It wasn't pretty.

The man was flat on his back. Her aunt's dog—not *her* dog, she'd be clear about that—was nosing through the guy's stuff, which must have flown out of his duffel bag in the melee.

"Bandit! Get back here! Right now!"

Excellent retriever that he was, her aunt's dog snatched up the Frisbee and streaked toward her, leaving the guy in the dust…er, sand.

"Hey! Bring that back!" Anger nipped at the man's voice as he righted himself, yanked down his T-shirt and slammed on a pair of sunglasses.

Bandit bounded up, tail wagging, and sat at her feet—holding a flipper that was the same color as the Frisbee.

Great.

But, hey. Anyone could make a mistake, right? The flipper looked a lot like the Frisbee at first glance. Sort of. To a dog. Maybe.

Somehow, though, Rachel doubted the man striding toward her was going to see it that way.

Especially since he'd just been flattened by the dog in question.

Better to jump in fast and get the apologies over before he reamed her about losing control of her dog and threatened a lawsuit for bodily injuries. Although other than that bandage on his knee, he appeared to be in fine condition.

Her gaze lingered on the bandage. Dropped lower.

Wait.

It wasn't a bandage.

It wasn't even a real leg.

The man was wearing a prosthesis.

Good grief.

Her aunt's dog had tackled a man with one leg.

Was there any possible way she could transform herself into a sand crab and disappear into the beach?

As Rachel stared at his leg, a blue Frisbee held by long, lean, sun-browned fingers appeared in her field of vision.

She jerked her head up, heat rising on her cheeks.

Smart move, Rachel. Add insult to injury by gawking.

"I think this is yours." He passed her the Frisbee.

She couldn't read his eyes behind his dark glasses, but she had no trouble deciphering his tone.

He was ticked.

Big-time.

Clenching the fingers of one hand around the edge of the disk, she leaned down, took the flipper from Bandit and handed it over. "Look…I'm really sorry about this. Are you hurt?"

"I've had more painful falls."

Her first instinct was to glance back at his leg.

She quashed it.

"That flipper does look kind of like a Frisbee." She aimed a distracted wave toward the appendage in his hand.

"A swim *fin* doesn't look anything like a Frisbee."

At his correction, her chin lifted a notch. Flipper, fin, who cared? "Maybe it does to a dog. And for the record, Bandit is very friendly. But when he's focused on retrieving, he tends to be oblivious to everything else."

The man regarded the dog. "Bandit. An apt name. I can see why you picked it."

Rachel appraised him. Was that a touch of amusement in his voice?

Maybe.

She softened her tone. "Actually, he belongs to my great-aunt. So on behalf of both her and Bandit, I apologize again. You're sure you're not hurt?" Hard as she tried, she couldn't keep her gaze from flicking down to his leg.

The sudden stiffening of his posture was subtle but unmistakable. "I'm fine. But you might want to keep that guy on a leash around kids. A forty-pound child wouldn't have fared as well." He leaned down and patted Bandit, but his cool tone suggested he was far less willing to forgive her faux pas. "And for the record," he parroted her own words back at her, "I'm no more prone to injury than a man who has two good legs."

With that, he turned away and headed toward his towel.

Rachel watched his retreating back, fanning her burning cheeks with the Frisbee.

That had gone really well.

Bandit nudged her leg, and she looked down at her canine friend. At least her aunt's dog liked her.

"Sorry, big guy. I think we'd better cool it for a while."

Tail drooping, he skulked back to the beach chair and flopped down, chin on paws, angled away from her—the same cold treatment she'd gotten from the other occupant of the beach, who was packing up his gear to make a fast exit.

With a sigh, Rachel trudged back to her chair and sat. As she did, one of the slats emitted an ominous crack.

Three seconds later, she found herself sprawled on the sand, staring up at the dark clouds invading the blue sky.

And hoping her rocky start to this year's vacation wasn't an omen of things to come.

Why in the world had he gotten so bent out of shape because some stranger had been taken aback by his prosthesis?

Jack Fletcher strode toward his SUV, stabbed the remote on his key clip and tossed his beach gear into the backseat.

After two and a half years, he should be past all that. He *was* past all that. It had been months since an awkward or uncomfortable or shocked reaction had rankled him.

So what had happened back on the beach just now?

He slid into the driver's seat, started the engine and cranked up the air. Instead of putting the car in gear, however, he rested his arms on the wheel and considered that question.

Most of the women he'd socialized with since re-entering the dating game a year ago had never suspected he had a prosthesis. Why would they? After months of painful practice, he'd mastered a natural gait. And the couple of women he'd told—the ones who'd seemed as if they might have potential for more than a few laughs on a Friday or Saturday night—hadn't appeared to be too bothered by the news.

Then again, they'd already known him when he'd dropped the bombshell. He'd made certain of that.

Too bad he hadn't had an opportunity to lay the same groundwork with the woman on the beach.

Expelling an annoyed breath, he shifted the SUV into drive. What did it matter, anyway? His mission here was straightforward and twofold: help Gram until she regained use of her broken wrist and try to keep his clients happy, despite the remote location. That was more than enough to occupy him for the next six or eight weeks. Impressing a shapely blonde with a friendly dog wasn't part of the plan.

Besides, the woman had been wearing a wedding ring. In all likelihood, she was here for a short family vacation. Maybe she'd dropped her kids at the Sea Turtle Center for one of the youth programs and decided to grab a few rays while her husband played golf. Assuming she was like most Jekyll Island visitors, she'd be gone in a week.

If he was smart, he'd forget about her.

Fletch pulled onto the main drag—such as it was—and pointed his SUV back toward Gram's. Not a single car passed him as he cruised down the island's two-lane circular road…a nice change from the Norfolk traffic. And in less than five minutes, he was swinging into the driveway of the tidy cottage Gram now called home. The short distances between destinations were also nice.

He set the brake, snagged his duffel bag and exited into the heat. All was quiet in this octogenarian neighborhood. That, too, was welcome. He'd heard enough loud noises to last a lifetime.

Still…this island's gentle, laid-back nature could drive someone who was used to action stir-crazy— unless there was an interesting diversion or two.

Like an attractive blonde.

Not going to happen, Fletcher. Suck it up and just do your duty.

Duty.

A twinge of regret echoed in his soul as he closed the car door and started for the house. Duty…obligation…responsibility—yeah, he knew all about those. They were part of Navy SEAL DNA, on and off the job. Forever.

He stepped up onto Gram's porch on his artificial leg.

He was here for the duration. That's how SEALs operated. They didn't let people down. No matter the cost.

"Did you have a pleasant time, dear?"

Rachel pushed through the outside door to the screen porch and dropped her tote bag onto a wicker chair before responding to her great-aunt's greeting. "It doesn't get much better than an afternoon on a Jekyll Island beach."

"True enough. Why do you think I moved here twelve years ago?"

She surveyed the woman across from her. Eleanor Kavanagh's driver's license might list her age as seventy-four, but one glance at her trim figure, wedge-cut blond hair and fashionable capris busted any stereotypical notions of the term *elderly.* "Don't you ever miss Cincinnati?"

Her aunt let loose with an unladylike snort. "Not a lick. I didn't have any complaints about my life there, mind you. I had a fine job that provided a steady income and a comfortable retirement—but being an accountant can't hold a candle to running an art gallery." She patted the retriever as he settled at her feet. "I see you kept Bandit dry."

"It was a struggle."

"I imagine." Her features softened as she stroked the dog. "Good thing I didn't go. Once he turns those dark brown eyes on me, I'm a goner. They're impossible to resist."

For some reason an image of the man from the beach materialized in Rachel's mind. Though his eyes had been hidden behind sunglasses, she had a feeling they were hard to resist, too.

"Rachel?"

She blinked and refocused on her aunt. "Sorry. I drifted for a minute."

"I noticed. I asked if there were many people on the beach."

"No. I had it almost to myself." She claimed one of the wicker rocking chairs on the porch.

"I thought you might. I've been sitting here for a while and I only saw one other person cross the access bridge over the dunes. He was leaving."

Rachel set the chair in motion. "Yes. I noticed him." No need to recount the whole incident with the Frisbee—or to mention her brief, charged interchange with the man.

"I couldn't get a clear look at him from this distance, but he seemed fairly young...from my perspective, at any rate." Her aunt swirled the ice in her glass of lemonade. "I don't see many solitary young men around here. I wonder if he's married."

"No." At her immediate response, Rachel frowned. For some strange reason, the image of his bare left hand was clear in her mind. "I mean, he wasn't wearing a ring. But a lot of guys don't. His wife might have gone shopping."

"That's not a big draw here."

"True. There isn't a mall in sight."

"But we do have a century-old hotel that serves high tea and hosts croquet tournaments on the lawn, plus a wonderful restored historic district. I'll take charm over shopping any day."

"I'm with you." At least her aunt was off the subject of the muscular swimmer.

"Speaking of charm…from the glimpse I had, that young man appeared to be quite handsome. You must have gotten a close-up look, if you could check for a ring."

So much for any hope of changing the subject.

As warmth rose on her cheeks, Rachel leaned down to brush a few grains of sand off one of her flip-flops. "I didn't check for a ring. I just happened to notice his bare hand when we exchanged a few words." Maybe Aunt El wouldn't spot the telltale flush.

No such luck.

"I do believe you might have gotten a bit too much sun." Eleanor appraised her. "Your face is pink.

Remember to take it easy for the first few days, until you get acclimated. And don't forget the sunscreen."

"Duly noted. With my fair complexion, I make liberal use of it at home in Richmond, too."

Her aunt dismissed that comment with a wave. "Sun in the city and sun on the beach are two very different things. That young man certainly had a nice tan."

Oh, brother.

Rising, Rachel reached for her tote bag. "I think I'll go ahead and change. I have to be at the hotel in an hour."

"When's your first program?"

"Next week."

"You've only been here two days—I wish you'd take some time to unwind before you dive into work again. That's why I didn't schedule you at the gallery right away."

Rachel slung her tote bag over her shoulder and bent down to pet Bandit as she passed. "I'll have a week off. Any more downtime, and I'd go crazy. Besides, I love being around children, so it's hardly work. And I'm used to being busy."

"Too busy, if you ask me."

"Busy is good."

"Not when it's an excuse." Her aunt gave her a shrewd look over the rim of her lemonade glass as she took a sip.

Straightening up, Rachel planted one hand on her hip. "For what?"

"Getting on with your life."

She exhaled slowly. This was not a discussion she wanted to have during this vacation—but her aunt's serious expression told her that while she might be able to escape it today, the topic was going to come up again.

"I have gotten on with my life. I have a great job helping kids discover their inner artist. I'm active at church. I have a lovely circle of friends. I prefer to think of my life as full rather than busy."

Her aunt watched her for a moment. "When's the last time you went on a date?"

Ah. So that's what this was about. She should have guessed. Aunt El had dropped a few subtle hints last summer about the importance of romance, which she'd ignored. But there was a disconcerting determination in her manner this year.

Perhaps it wasn't going to be such a relaxing summer after all.

"It's only been three years, Aunt El." She tightened her grip on the strap of the tote bag, her voice subdued. "Someday I might go down that road again. But I've only just begun to entertain that idea. I'm nowhere near ready to act on it."

Eleanor took another sip of her lemonade. "Well, you know best, of course. I just don't want to see you end up alone. The way you love children, you should have a houseful of your own."

A twinge of pain echoed in her heart. That had been the plan, once upon a time. But she and Mark had barely gotten past the launch stage.

She didn't want to talk about that, either.

"Maybe it's not in the cards."

"The only way to find out is to play the game."

Time to go on the offensive.

"But you never married, and you've always been perfectly happy."

For one tiny second, a shadow darkened Eleanor's eyes, come and gone so fast Rachel would have thought she'd imagined it—except for her aunt's next words.

"I've been happy because I chose to be. Sometimes you have to accept what life hands you and make the best of it. But if I'd had the chance to marry and create a family, I'd have done it in a heartbeat."

Rachel stared at her, speechless. Everyone in the family had always assumed Aunt El had been a confirmed bachelorette from the get-go. Spunky, independent, smart, witty—she'd always been viewed by the female side of the family as proof a woman alone could march to the beat of her own drummer and lead a joy-filled, productive life.

"I didn't know that. I'm sorry you never met the right man."

A whisper of sadness echoed in the depths of Eleanor's eyes. "I didn't say that."

Rachel cocked her head. "What do you mean?"

The sadness evaporated, and Eleanor was once again her upbeat, no-nonsense self. "That's a story for another day, my dear. You best get ready for your meeting at the hotel."

A few minutes ago, Rachel had been anxious to break away from her aunt. Now she hesitated, her curiosity piqued.

Eleanor's eyes began to twinkle. "You know, we all have our secrets, good and bad. Close as the two of us have always been, I daresay you haven't told me all of yours, either…old *or* new."

Her encounter with the man on the beach replayed through her mind, and once again her neck warmed.

"I thought so." Eleanor sent her a smug look.

She was out of there.

"I'll be back in time for dinner." Rachel called the comment over her shoulder as she flip-flopped into the house. How in the world had they gotten on the subject of secrets?

And what secrets did her aunt harbor?

Yet as she dropped her tote on the bed and selected an outfit to wear to the hotel, thoughts of Aunt El's secrets gave way to the solitary man on the beach. A tanned, fit swimmer with an artificial leg and no wedding ring who wouldn't have given her a second look if Bandit hadn't intervened.

We all have our secrets, good and bad.

What secrets did he have? Were they mostly good…or bad?

She pulled the puckered seersucker sundress from its hanger, running her fingers over the alternating rows of textured stripes. Smooth, bumpy, smooth, bumpy. Kind of like life—smooth patches followed by lots of bumps and wrinkles.

Based on his artificial leg, the guy at the beach had had his share of rough patches. Maybe more than his share. What had happened to him? Why was he alone? What had brought him to Jekyll Island?

Shaking her head, Rachel tossed the dress on the bed and detoured to the bathroom to touch up her French braid. She needed to switch gears and psyche herself up for her meeting with the new activities director at the Jekyll Island Club Hotel. She hadn't come here to think about strangers on a beach or dates or whether her busy…*full*…schedule at home was healthy.

She'd come here to relax.

And neither her aunt's prodding nor an unsettling encounter on the beach were going to interfere with that plan.

Chapter Two

"Did you have any problem finding the beach access?"

As Louise Fletcher stepped from the house to the patio, a plate of cookies in hand, Fletch tried not to stare. Last time he'd come for a visit, his grandmother had been her usual self—short hair neatly coiffed in the tight curls she'd always favored, sensible flat shoes, modest-length dark skirt and crisp blouse.

Now she looked like an aging hippie. What was with the spiky blow-dried hair and the bare feet and the floor-length muumuu thing?

"Young man, you've been inspecting me like I'm an alien ever since you arrived yesterday." She set the plate of cookies on the table beside him and eased into the adjacent chair, cradling the cast on her left wrist. "What's the problem?"

That direct approach was new, too. Gram used to be much more soft-spoken and discreet.

Clearing his throat, he helped himself to a cookie. "You just look a lot different than when I came for Thanksgiving."

"I should hope so. It took me a while, but I finally got with the program."

"What program?" He took a bite of the cookie, letting the warm chocolate chips dissolve on his tongue. At least one thing hadn't changed. His grandmother's baking skills were still top-notch—though how she'd managed to make these one-handed, he had no idea.

"This is island living, my boy. We're casual here. Throw out the girdle. Throw out the pantyhose. Throw out the curlers. I might be seventy-seven, but I'm not too old to learn a few new tricks."

Aiming a dubious look her direction, Fletch shoved another cookie in his mouth.

"What?"

"You're…different. That's all."

"I prefer the word *better*."

"I'm not sure about that."

"I am—and that's all that counts."

Truth be told, her new feistiness was kind of a hoot. She and Gramp had enjoyed a long and happy marriage, but she'd really come into her own in widowhood and done things he'd never expected. Like taking that around-the-world cruise on a freighter a year ago, then moving here last fall without consulting anyone.

Not that he was certain he approved of this latest

adventure. She was almost eighty, after all, and the closest hospital was miles away, on the mainland.

But Gram didn't need his approval. She liked the changes in her life, and she was right—that was all that counted.

Even if this latest one had produced a broken wrist.

As if reading his mind, Gram leaned forward and fixed him with an intent look. "Now see here, young man." The slight Southern twang of her Nashville roots was another thing that hadn't changed. "I could have tripped over a shopping cart in any parking lot in any grocery store in this country. It just happened to be in Brunswick. And Eleanor Kavanagh, bless her soul, took fine care of me until you got here."

She settled back, her expression thoughtful. "Funny how you can go through your whole life and then, in the last stages, find the best friend you ever had." She shook her head. "All part of God's plan, I guess."

"I'm looking forward to seeing her again. We didn't have much chance to get acquainted at Thanksgiving."

"You can say hello at church on Sunday. You're going to services, aren't you?"

Fletch shifted and gave the task of selecting his next cookie more attention than it deserved. "No, but I'll be happy to drop you off."

"Still at odds with the Almighty, I see."

He settled on a cookie he no longer wanted. "Let it go, Gram."

Several beats of silence ticked by.

"We don't have to discuss it if you don't want to—but I intend to keep praying. And I can get a ride with Eleanor to church. So…you never answered my question. Did you have any problem finding the beach access?"

He leaned back in his chair. Good. She'd let the subject of his lapsed faith drop—for now. "No. Your directions were excellent. I would never have guessed there were access points tucked into the residential streets."

"Most people wouldn't. That's why those beaches are usually empty. Did you have it all to yourself?"

"Almost." Fletch chewed the cookie, visualizing the blonde. "I only had to share it with a woman and her dog."

"That sounds about right. I walked that beach every day before I broke this," she wiggled the fingers protruding from the cast, "and I never saw more than a couple of people. They were always friendly, though. Seems like beaches bring out the best in people. Did you have an opportunity to chat with her?"

Their brief exchange didn't qualify as a chat, and as for friendly…not even close.

"I went there to swim, not talk." He washed down the last of the cookie with a swig of soda.

Twin furrows creased her brow. "I hope you're not turning into a recluse."

One side of his mouth hiked up. "Trust me, Gram. The accident might have sidelined me for a few months, but in the past year I've led an active social life."

The furrows diminished a bit. "So in other words, you're just waiting for the right woman to come along."

It wasn't quite that simple…but close enough for this discussion.

"More or less."

Her forehead smoothed out. "Nice to know. Because your brother doesn't seem in any hurry to get married, and I want to enjoy some grandbabies before the good Lord calls me home."

Fletch's fingers tightened on the empty aluminum can, the crinkling noise echoing in the sudden silence. After a moment, he set it on the patio table, pulled his cell off his belt and stood. "I need to return a call. Would you like me to take the cookies inside?"

"Please. Otherwise, I'll eat too many—and I made them for you. That's not a chore I plan to tackle again until this comes off, by the way." She lifted her cast. "So enjoy them."

"I appreciate the effort." Fletch bent down and kissed her forehead. "But no more heavy cooking. I can take over a lot of the KP while I'm here. It won't be up to your standards, but we'll get by."

She waved the offer aside. "I can prepare simple things. The least I can do is feed you after disrupting your life. I don't know what I'd have done if your work wasn't portable."

"Well, it is and I'll manage fine with the island as a temporary base." Not quite true, but no need to lay any guilt on Gram about the inconvenience.

"You have to promise me you'll build in some social time, though. I don't expect you to wait on me hand and foot. Besides, you're not getting any younger. You need to think about settling down and starting a family."

Gram's new lifestyle might be casual and laid-back, but she clearly hadn't dialed down her determination see him married.

"Thirty-five isn't exactly over the hill."

"No…but you don't want to be dealing with night feedings and diapers in your forties if you can help it."

Fletch forced his lips into the semblance of a smile. "I'll keep that in mind."

Juggling the plate of cookies in his hand, he reentered the house. Only then did he allow the corners of his mouth to flatten.

Gram was right.

He wasn't getting any younger.

But he had secrets she didn't know. Guilt that ate at his soul. Grief that remained raw after two and a half years.

It would take a very special woman to deal with all the baggage he carried.

And so far, he was batting zero.

Leaving him less than upbeat that his chances were going to improve anytime soon.

As Eleanor slowed the car to a stop on a tiny lane that bisected the interior of the island, she gestured toward a small bungalow. "That's Louise's house."

Rachel surveyed the well-kept cottage, the tidy yard and the flower-rimmed sidewalk that led to the front door. "It's charming. How's she adjusting to island life?"

"After only eight months, you'd think she was a native. Took to it like a duck to water. I knew she would the day we met at church." Eleanor glanced from her watch to the door. "That broken wrist must be slowing her down, though. Louise is always punctual—and she hates to be late for services."

"Would you like me to ring the bell?"

Eleanor tapped her finger on the steering wheel. "I suppose it couldn't hurt. Maybe she could use a hand with a zipper or something."

"No problem. We should be fine. The church is only five minutes from here."

Her aunt chuckled. "Everything's five minutes from here."

"Good point. I'll be back in a sec." Grinning,

Rachel slid out, followed the path to the door and pressed the bell.

Fifteen seconds ticked by.

She tried again.

Another fifteen seconds passed.

A flicker of alarm nudged up her pulse.

Had Louise fallen again? Was she ill? Had she forgotten Aunt El's offer of a ride and made other arrangements? Should they…

At the sound of a lock sliding on the other side of the door, she exhaled. There wasn't a problem after all.

As the knob turned, Rachel lightened her expression, prepared to greet her aunt's new best friend… and froze.

What on earth was the man from the beach doing here?

While she stared at him, he stared back.

She found her voice first. "We meet again."

He looked past her, toward the car where Aunt El waited. "I take it you're somehow connected to Eleanor."

"Great-niece. I take it you're connected to Louise."

"Grandson."

She tried to think of something else to say. Failed.

He seemed to be having the same problem.

"Is that you, Rachel?" Louise's cheery greeting sounded from within the house, and a moment later she hurried into view.

Once again Rachel found herself staring.

Was this flower-child senior with the mod hair, funky sandals and colorful knee-length caftanlike garment the same quiet, conservatively dressed woman who'd shared Christmas dinner with her and Aunt El?

The woman gathered her into a one-handed hug as Rachel tried to process the transformation.

"Let me look at you." Louise backed off to scrutinize her. "Pretty as a picture, just like I remember. How do you like the new me?" She did a pirouette, her eyes twinkling.

"Um…it's different." Rachel studied the older woman. "But I like it."

Louise laughed. "The very thing Fletch said. The different part, anyway. I'm not sure he's sold on the updates, but life's full of surprises, isn't it? By the way, let me introduce you two."

"We've met." The swimmer's face was unreadable.

"Is that right?" Louise swiveled her head from one to the other.

Since the man in question didn't seem inclined to offer any more information, Rachel spoke up. "We ran into each other at the beach on Wednesday."

"Literally." He folded his arms. "Her dog knocked me down."

"*Aunt El's* dog," Rachel corrected.

Louise's eyes widened. "Rachel was the woman with the dog you mentioned?"

"Small world, I guess." Fletch leaned a shoulder against the door.

"True enough. Especially on Jekyll Island." Louise beamed at him. "Now isn't this nice? Two young people at loose ends for the summer."

Her grandson straightened up at once, annoyance tightening his features. "I'm not at loose ends, Gram. When I'm not helping you, I'll be working."

"Not 24/7."

Warmth stole onto Rachel's cheeks. It was obvious to her, if not to Louise, that this Fletch guy had zero interest in her. And that was fine. If she ever decided to go out on a date again, it would be with someone who wanted to spend time with her, not someone shoved her direction by an overeager if well-meaning relation.

And he'd been shoved, no question about it. Why else would he have shown up on Aunt El's beach, halfway around the island, when there were perfectly fine beaches much closer?

If his sudden scowl was any indication, he'd come to the same conclusion.

As the silence lengthened, Rachel edged away from the door—and the man. "I think we'd better leave or we'll miss the opening hymn."

Louise consulted her watch. "Goodness, you're right. Fletch, are you certain I can't convince you to come?"

"Yes."

No hesitation there. An aversion to church—or to her?

Rachel straightened her shoulders and crooked her elbow. "Why don't you take my arm, Louise, just to be safe?"

"Don't mind if I do. It doesn't hurt to be extra careful until I ditch this thing." Louise lifted the cast. "I'll be back in a couple of hours, Fletch."

"No rush. I've got some work to do."

Louise shot him a pointed look. "In my day, people didn't work on Sundays."

"Times change." Fletch edged the door closed as Louise exited, as if he couldn't be rid of them fast enough.

"And not always for the better." The door clicked shut before his grandmother finished her reply. She frowned at the closed door. "Now where are that boy's manners? He didn't even say goodbye to you."

Rachel guided her down the walk. "Maybe he has a lot on his mind." *Or he's just plain rude.*

The latter seemed more than plausible.

"That doesn't excuse bad manners. I'll have to have a talk with him after I get back."

Rachel rolled her eyes. That would go over real well. Louise's grandson struck her as a take-charge kind of guy who wouldn't appreciate criticism. A scolding from his grandmother wasn't likely to endear Eleanor's niece to him.

But who cared? There was no reason for their

paths to cross again. Now that they were both on to his grandmother's—and perhaps Aunt El's—transparent beach strategy, he'd no doubt get his rays elsewhere. It didn't sound as if she'd run into him at church, either. Nor did he seem like the gallery-visiting type, so the odds he'd stop in to Aunt El's shop were nil. They could each go their separate ways and spend their summers exactly as they'd intended.

Everything was good.

Rachel helped Louise into the front passenger seat, glancing back at the older woman's cottage as she reached for the back door. For one tiny instant, she thought she detected a shadow at the window, as if someone had been watching them. Not much chance of that, though, given the man's reaction to her today—and on the beach.

But if everything was good, how was she supposed to explain the little wave of disappointment that suddenly dimmed her spirits?

Fletch finished setting the table and strolled over to the stove, giving the simmering pot an appreciative sniff as he stopped beside Gram. "That smells fantastic."

"Shrimp and scallop risotto. It's one of my staples these days—but I must say, it's wonderful to have someone to share it with." Gram added more liquid to the mixture and continued to stir. "You missed a fine sermon today, by the way. Reverend Carlson talked about…" The jingle of the phone cut her off.

"Want me to get that?"

She shot a dark look toward the portable in its cradle. "If you wouldn't mind. Risotto needs constant attention."

He moved down to the other end of the counter, grateful for the reprieve from a recap of the minister's remarks, and picked up the remote. After exchanging hellos with Eleanor, he carried the phone back to his grandmother and held it out. "She says it's important."

Gram shoved the heavy spoon into his hand. "Keep stirring or the rice will sink and stick to the bottom and we'll end up with a burned mess instead of dinner."

Without waiting for a reply, she took the phone and greeted her friend.

Leaning one shoulder against the adjacent wall, Fletch kept the spoon moving as Gram talked.

"No, I have a minute. I put Fletch in charge of the risotto." In the silence that followed, her brow wrinkled. "Oh, my. That *is* a problem. We were counting on them."

More silence as she paced over to the rear window by the sink. Although she looked out, Fletch had a feeling she wasn't seeing the stately live oak dripping with Spanish moss that dominated her backyard.

"Yes, I do understand. These things happen."

Gram sighed. "I guess we'll have to cancel the second half of the summer, too. Everyone will be so disappointed."

Fletch continued to stir as Gram went back into listening mode. As he watched, she caught her bottom lip between her teeth, and her expression shifted from troubled to pensive. "Yes, I see what you're saying. Everything does happen for a reason." More silence. "That sounds like a plan. I'll touch base with you tomorrow morning and put the committee meeting on my calendar for tomorrow night at seven. Talk to you soon."

After replacing the handset in the cradle, she rejoined him at the stove.

"Problems?" He handed the spoon back to her.

"Yes. Such a shame." Gram leaned close to the pot to gauge his diligence with the risotto, gave a satisfied nod and resumed stirring. "Last year, around Thanksgiving, some of us in the congregation got to talking about how Jekyll Island is such a wonderful family vacation spot. We thought it would be lovely to see if we could find a fixer-upper island house for sale, refurbish it and then invite twelve needy families to come for a week's stay each summer." She gestured toward the refrigerator. "Would you mind handing me the bowl of scallops and shrimp on the second shelf?"

"Not if that means I get to eat soon. My salivary

glands are working overtime." He crossed to the refrigerator and found the bowl.

"It'll only be four minutes once I add those." She gestured toward the bowl in his hands.

He pulled off the plastic wrap and rejoined her. "Want me to dump them in?"

"Yes, thanks. This one-handed thing is getting old."

Once that task was completed, she went back to stirring and picked up her story. "Anyway, an older gentleman who lived on the island died last winter, not long after the congregation formed a committee to investigate the idea. He hadn't updated his house in years, and since his family was eager to sell, things moved quickly. We got it at a bargain price, so we had enough donations to cover the full cost of the house. But the plan was for members of the congregation to do most of the renovation work. Then our retired carpenter had to have his hip replaced. Our retired electrician had a heart attack. Now I've broken my wrist."

Fletch leaned back against the counter and folded his arms across his chest. "It almost sounds like the project is jinxed."

Gram sent him a stern look. "Don't even say such a thing. Of course it's not jinxed. It's a wonderful project that could do a world of good for a lot of families. We've had a few setbacks is all. We got way behind on our timetable, and we had to cancel the reservations for the first six families. Still, we were confident we could wrap things up by mid-July."

"But…?"

She sighed. "Eleanor's the chairwoman of the committee, and she just got a call from the youngest couple in our group who we were relying on for some of the heavier cosmetic stuff—stripping wallpaper, painting, cleaning grout…that kind of thing. They're only in their early sixties and much more agile than some of us. But her parents are in their late eighties, and her father's had some sort of medical crisis. So they're going back to Michigan for a few weeks." She passed the spoon to him again. "That pot's too heavy for me to deal with one-handed. Would you dish this up while I get our drinks?"

"Sure." They switched places, and he scooped generous portions onto plates as she filled glasses with water and added a platter of sliced tomatoes to the table.

By the time he joined her and settled into his seat, she'd taken her place, as well.

"So the project is at a standstill." He draped his napkin over his lap and picked up his fork.

"Not quite, but progress will be slow. I'm afraid we'll have to cancel the remaining reservations." Distress tightened her features. "I hate to disappoint those families, but I don't know what else we can do. Let's pray about it, shall we?"

His fork froze in midair, the aroma of the risotto

tantalizing his nostrils. With a concerted effort, he forced it back to his plate.

Gram bowed her head. "Lord, we thank You for this wonderful food and for family ties. We thank You for allowing us to call this beautiful spot in Your creation home, whether for a lifetime or for a vacation. We pray that You'll allow our church to find a way to give this gift of beauty and respite to the deserving families who need a break from the daily grind and who may also be in need of an infusion of hope. Guide us, Lord, and inspire us so that we can find a solution to this dilemma. Amen."

Fletch picked up his fork again and dove into the risotto, which was every bit as tasty as the aroma had promised.

"This is great, Gram." He wedged in the compliment as he shoveled in forkfuls of the hearty concoction.

"I'm glad you like it. That was another thing we were going to do for our guests—take turns providing meals. I was planning to make this for dinner one night each week for the family in residence. I figured it would be an upscale treat for most of them. Our pastor sifted through candidates he gathered from his clerical friends in economically troubled parts of the South, and they've all had some tough breaks. I expect most of them subsist on very basic fare. It reminded me how very blessed people like you and I are to have plentiful food on the table every night."

Fletch slowed his pace. Gram was right—and he too often took his comfortable life for granted. "I'm sorry about the program. It sounds very worthwhile. Maybe some sort of solution will present itself and you won't have to cancel out on the rest of the people."

"Trust me, I'm adding that to my prayer list."

He half expected her to ask him to pray, too—but she didn't. Perhaps she'd finally reconciled herself to the fact that her grandson and God had parted ways.

Still…he hoped God listened to the devout woman across from him, who'd always had such a firm belief in the power of prayer.

And he hoped He gave her exactly what she asked for.

Chapter Three

As Rachel finished emptying the dishwasher, Aunt El pushed through the door from the attached garage, a thick file folder in hand. "Thank you for taking care of that, dear. I didn't expect the meeting to run this late or to have to eat early and leave you on your own for dinner."

"I wasn't on my own. I had Bandit for company."

At the mention of his name, the golden retriever appeared from the living room and padded straight for Eleanor, who stroked his head.

Rachel wiped her hands on a dishtowel. The usual sparkle in her aunt's eyes had dimmed a few watts, and there was a slight slump to her shoulders. Even before she asked the question, she had a feeling she knew the answer. "How did it go?"

Eleanor set the folder on the glass-topped kitchen table and sighed. "Not great. If we had any additional money, we could pay people to do the renovations.

But we needed every penny in the fund to buy the house, even though the sellers gave us a great deal and took part of the value as a tax write-off. With some of our key volunteers sidelined, we just don't have the manpower to get the job done."

"I'm sorry. I know how important this project is to you."

"Thank you, my dear." Her aunt patted her hand. "I guess I'll make the cancellation calls to the rest of the families in the morning, between customers at the gallery. Right now, I believe I'll take a bath and call it a night. Are you all set for your first program tomorrow?"

"Yes. Organizing the art supplies I hauled down from Richmond and getting the lay of the land at the hotel were my priorities today."

"Did you work in any beach time?"

"A couple of hours—only because Bandit made me go."

The golden retriever looked up at her and wagged his tail.

"Good for him. R&R is wonderful for the soul. Did you see Fletch again?" A spark of interest kindled in the older woman's eyes.

"No. He probably found a beach closer to Louise's house."

This was the perfect opportunity to discuss last week's obvious setup…but in light of the problems her aunt was dealing with, Rachel didn't have the heart to bring it up. Besides, it was a moot point. If she'd read him correctly on Sunday, Louise's grandson had been as miffed about their respective relatives' manipulation as she was—which had flopped, in any case. There wasn't much chance he'd want anything further to do with the rude woman who'd gawked at his artificial leg and sicced a seventy-pound dog on him.

"I suppose so." Eleanor positioned the folder in the middle of the table, opened it and riffled through the sheaf of papers. "Such a pity to disappoint so many people." She expelled a long breath and turned away. "Waffles at eight?"

"You don't have to spoil me. A bowl of cereal is fine."

"Nonsense. You can eat cereal at home. A visit to Jekyll Island should be filled with special treats." Her aunt winked. "But if it makes you feel better, I'm glad to have an excuse to eat real breakfasts myself for a few weeks a year. The rest of the time I subsist on cereal, too."

They had the same conversation every summer, and as usual, Rachel capitulated. "In that case…I'll look forward to it."

"In the meantime, sweet dreams. Bandit, are you coming?"

The dog rose from his sitting position and trotted after his owner.

As Eleanor disappeared down the hall, Rachel

drummed her fingers against the countertop. It wasn't even ten yet. Too early for bed and too dark to go for a walk on the beach. TV held no appeal, and if she dived back into the taut thriller she'd taken to the beach earlier she'd stay up far too late reading just one more page.

Maybe she'd end the day with a soothing cup of herbal tea.

Choosing a bag from her aunt's large selection, she eyed the folder on the table. It was a shame about the church project—though she'd always thought it too ambitious for the aging congregation. Still, she couldn't fault their generous spirit. They were living the values Reverend Carlson preached from the pulpit every Sunday and doing God's work.

So why had He allowed obstacle after obstacle to disrupt their efforts to serve Him?

She tossed the bag in a mug, answers about the Almighty eluding her, as usual.

But she wasn't going to let herself grow bitter. She would cling to the belief that He had plans for her welfare, not her woe. Plans to give her a future full of hope. Holding fast to that verse from Jeremiah was what had gotten her through the losses. That, and the love and support Aunt El had offered once her parents and brother had returned to their far-flung homes.

After filling the mug with water, she set it in the microwave, strolled back to the table, and leaned over to examine the contents of the open file. Twelve sets of stapled documents were on top, each containing two or three pages. The six at the back were held together with a binder clip. Those must be the people who'd already lost their chance to visit Jekyll, based on the arrival dates noted at the top of the cover sheets.

Rachel refocused on the set at the top of the pile. It was background information on the family slated to participate in the program beginning on July 14—in less than five weeks.

Joseph and Sarah Mitchell, ages thirty-seven and thirty-four, and their four children—Aaron, nine; Nicole, seven; Angela, four; Peter, six months. Joseph was an IT technician who'd been out of work for eight months…a victim of overseas outsourcing, according to the write-up from his minister. Hardworker, regular churchgoer, loving father, devoted husband—the accolades were abundant. He was taking odd jobs to make ends meet, but they were struggling. On top of all that, they'd lost their oldest son in a bicycle accident a year ago. The stress had extracted a toll on everyone, and the family was in desperate need of a brief respite.

The microwave beeped, and Rachel wandered back to retrieve her tea.

If every story in the file was that heartrending, it was no wonder the sparkle in her aunt's eyes had flagged at the thought of having to deliver more bad news to families who'd already borne more than their share of difficulty.

Dipping the bag in the hot water, Rachel returned to the table. A quick scan of the remaining sets of pages confirmed her suspicion. Every family in the file could benefit from a relaxing, carefree week on Jekyll Island.

As she sipped her tea, the warmth in the ceramic mug seeped into her fingers—just as the stories of these deserving families had seeped into her heart.

Was there anything she could do to keep more of them from being disappointed? She wasn't a carpenter or an electrician or a plumber, but she could wield a mean paintbrush, knew how to rip up carpeting and wasn't afraid of heavy-duty cleaning.

Would that kind of contribution make a difference? Not likely.

But first thing tomorrow, before Aunt El left for the gallery, she'd offer anyway.

And even if her efforts wouldn't be enough to prevent more cancellations, she'd still pitch in. Because helping with a worthwhile project this summer suddenly held a whole lot more appeal than spending her free time lying on the beach.

"You're up early."

As Gram entered the kitchen, Fletch finished typing the email, hit the send button and angled his wrist. Seven already? Somehow he'd lost track of the time. "I have a client in Europe who burns the midnight oil. I've been back and forth with him since four-thirty."

Gram's eyes widened. "Mercy! Do you always keep such odd hours?"

Odd hours? After military life, when he'd often gone two full days with no shut-eye while dodging bullets and freezing on a harsh mountainside, getting up at four-thirty didn't qualify as odd. "Not always. I made coffee, if you want some." He gestured toward the half-empty pot on the counter.

"I see you've already put quite a dent in it." She moved across the room. "I heard you typing in your room after I got home last night, too. What time did you get to bed?"

"Around eleven-thirty."

"Five hours of sleep isn't enough."

"It is for me." Especially when nightmares plagued his slumber. "So how did your meeting go?"

She filled a mug and joined him at the table, frowning. "I think we're hosed."

His lips twitched. Gram using urban slang—another first. What other surprises would this trip hold?

He covered his amused reaction by taking a sip of coffee, then grimaced at the tepid brew. As he rose for a warm-up, he spoke over his shoulder. "How much would it take to get things up and running?"

When Gram didn't reply at once, he topped off

his mug and turned to find her regarding him with an expression he couldn't read. "What?"

"Are you thinking of making a contribution?"

"Maybe—if it will wipe that frown off your face."

Instead of disappearing, the indentations on her forehead deepened. "I wasn't angling for your money."

"I know, but I have some excess cash and it sounds like a worthy cause."

A few beats of silence ticked by as Gram stirred some cream into her coffee. He could almost hear the gears grinding in her brain. "That's a very generous offer. But you should be putting your extra money into a house fund of your own for when you have a family."

That wasn't the response he'd expected.

He tightened his grip on his mug. "That could be a long way off. The need you have is more immediate."

She tapped a finger on the polished oak tabletop. "I'll tell you what. Let me call Eleanor at a more decent hour and see what she thinks. In the meantime, I'll give you some information on the families who are scheduled to come. If you're thinking about investing in the project, you ought to have some idea of who's going to benefit." She started to rise.

"That's not necessary. If you and your church think this is worth doing, I'll take your word for it."

She kept moving. "I'd feel better if you gave the file a quick read. Writing a check for charity is all well and good, but it means more if you know who you're helping."

Before Fletch could reiterate his protest, Gram had already disappeared down the hall.

Settling back in his chair, he opened the new email that had come in during their brief conversation. The project in Newark was heating up. They were going to want him on-site sooner rather than later for a walk-through. Could he make it a day trip so he didn't have to leave Gram alone at night, in case she needed help?

In truth, though, she seemed to be coping fine except for needing help with buttons and zippers and can openers. As for getting around, Eleanor appeared to be more than willing to act as a chauffeur when needed.

So why had she been so eager to have him come for an extended visit?

As he pondered that, Gram appeared in the doorway, crossed the room and set a file beside him. "Here you go. Why don't you take it down to the beach this afternoon and look through it after your swim? And if you run into Rachel, you might think about apologizing."

He arched an eyebrow. "For what?"

"You didn't even say goodbye to her yesterday when we left for church—let alone 'Nice to meet you.'"

That was true.

But since he didn't plan to see her again, what did it matter?

Not that Gram would buy that excuse.

"Sorry. My manners must have tarnished while I was overseas."

"Well, polish them up. You were raised better than that. And you'll need them if you want to attract a nice girl—like Rachel."

"I don't want to attract a nice girl like Rachel."

She sent him a surprised look. "Why ever not?"

"I prefer to date unmarried women."

She stared at him. "What on earth are you talking about?"

"Your friend's niece wears a wedding ring. I assume she's married."

Gram lifted her good hand to her cheek. "Oh, my. You're right, she does wear her ring. I'd completely forgotten about that. No wonder…"

When her voice trailed off, he tipped his head. "No wonder what?"

"Nothing." She fluttered her uninjured hand. "Just to clear things up, she's not married anymore. Her husband died."

His blond beach mate was a widow?

Three seconds of silence ticked by as he digested that bombshell.

"I should have told you that upfront, I guess." Gram patted his shoulder.

It was on the tip of his tongue to probe for details—but he bit back his questions as the light dawned.

The broken wrist might have been Gram's excuse for pushing him to visit, but she had a second agenda.

She and Eleanor had concocted some sort of plan to match up their two younger relations.

No wonder she'd insisted he visit the off-the-beaten-path beach on Sunday.

He sent her a narrow-eyed look. One fumbled attempt to pair up the two of them he could handle. But if she intended to launch some sort of intensive matchmaking campaign, he was out of there—broken wrist or no broken wrist.

As if sensing she was on thin ice, Gram leaned down and kissed his forehead. "I'll let you get back to work now...and I'll pass on Eleanor's input about your donation offer after I talk with her."

She opened the sliding glass door, making a production out of the one-handed maneuver—as if to remind him of her temporary disability. Then she carefully picked up her mug and exited. Once she was settled at the patio table, her cast resting on the arm of her chair, she paged through the newspaper on the table in front of her.

The picture of innocence.

Except Fletch wasn't buying it. He might not be certain who this new version of Gram really was, but he did know one thing.

Louise Fletcher had always been strong willed,

albeit in a quieter, more genteel way. When she set her mind on something, she could be as tenacious as a gull following one of the Jekyll Island fishing boats. And while other things about her may have changed since his previous visit, he suspected her determination was as formidable as ever.

On the plus side, at least she was transparent. Whatever plans she and Eleanor had cooked up to throw him and a certain blonde together could be thwarted. He was well versed in evasive maneuvers…and he'd have no qualms about using them.

Because the last thing he wanted to do was spend time with a woman who was fixated on his disability.

No matter how attractive she might be.

Rachel took a swig from her bottle of water and surveyed the large round table in the hotel conference room, where her eight enthusiastic charges were gluing the shells and other beach flotsam they'd gathered onto sturdy art boards.

This year's first "Art from the Sea" session was a rousing success.

Almost.

Her gaze shifted to six-year-old Madeleine on the far side of the table. From the get-go, the little girl with the solemn blue eyes and wispy strawberry blond ponytail had seemed indifferent. As the other children giggled and dashed about, collecting their treasures on the beach, Madeleine had trudged through the sand, eyes downcast, empty bucket in hand. If Rachel hadn't tucked a few shells in the bottom, the child would have had nothing to work with during the second half of the session.

As it was, she'd simply glued one small shell onto a corner of the board—and then, only when prompted.

Nor had she shown any interest in painting. Her watercolor consisted of a black horizon line with a gray sky and grayer water—even though the heavens and the sea had been a brilliant blue today.

"Rachel…shall I start cleaning things up?"

At the prompt from the college-age summer hotel employee who'd been assigned to assist with the session, she nodded. "Yes. Thanks, Lauren."

Bottle of water in hand, Rachel made one more circuit of the table, offering praise and encouragement. All the children beamed at her—except Madeleine. The little girl just sat quietly, fiddling with one of the unused shells in the small pile beside her.

Twenty minutes later, long after all of the other youngsters had been reclaimed by their parents, she was still sitting there.

Lauren finished clearing off the table, moved beside Rachel and spoke softly. "Would you like me to have the desk call her parents?" She gestured toward Madeleine.

"Yes. I'll stay with her until someone comes. I know you have other things to do."

Lauren grinned. "Lunch is first on the agenda."

"That's my next stop, too. I'll see you Thursday."

As her assistant disappeared out the door, Rachel slid into a seat next to Madeleine. "I'm sure your mommy or daddy will be here any minute, sweetie."

For a long moment, the child didn't respond. Then she raised her chin and looked up with sad eyes. "My daddy isn't here. And sometimes my mommy forgets about me."

While Rachel struggled to process that poignant comment and come up with a reply, Madeleine spoke again. "You can leave me at the front desk, if you want to. That's what people usually do. Mommy will look for me there." She tilted her head. "How come you know so much about painting and stuff?"

It took Rachel a few seconds to switch gears. "I'm an art teacher. Most of my students are just a couple of years older than you."

"Do you have any little girls or boys of your own?"

A jolt ripped through her at the unexpected question, twisting her stomach into an all-too-familiar knot. "No."

"How come?"

Her lungs stalled. She didn't talk about that subject. Ever. To anyone. "It's a long story."

The little girl heaved a sigh and poked at the shell she'd glued to the cardboard. "That's what grownups always say when they don't want to answer questions." The still-soft glue gave way, and the shell popped off the board, leaving the space empty.

Rachel plucked it from the floor, struggling to come up with a response as she pressed it back into position, trying to repair the child's artwork.

But a loud rumble from the youngster's stomach gave her an excuse to change the subject. "Are you hungry?"

Madeleine nodded.

"Let's see what I can find in my tote bag." As she reached for it, Rachel took a mental inventory. The children in today's class had been too occupied to think about food, so her snack supply was intact. Cheese crackers or a chocolate chip granola bar? She'd let Madeleine choose.

She rummaged around and pulled out the two items. Madeleine went straight for the salty snack.

By the time Rachel retrieved a bottle of water for her from the ice-filled tub on a side table, the girl had devoured half of the crackers. Twisting off the cap, Rachel retook her seat and set the bottle beside her. "What did you have for breakfast?"

"I dint hav brefus." The words came out garbled as she wolfed down another cracker.

Rachel frowned. No breakfast? That meant Madeleine hadn't eaten for fifteen hours, minimum.

What was wrong with this child's mother?

She fished another pack of crackers out of her bag and handed them over, doing her best to curb her anger at the blatant neglect. "Do you skip breakfast a lot?"

"Not at home. I eat at day care." She wrinkled her nose. "The food isn't real good, though. In hotels, I only eat if room service comes before we have to leave."

"It sounds like you travel around a lot."

"Mmm-hmm. Mommy has lots of meetings in different places. She has a very important job."

Apparently more important than feeding her child and picking her up on time.

As that thought flashed through her mind, the door to the conference room opened and a thin, thirty-something woman in business attire, cell phone in hand, pushed through. Once she spotted them, she held up one finger and continued her phone conversation.

"I need the revised data in thirty minutes, max. Email a new PowerPoint slide to illustrate it, and send as much backup as possible." Silence while she tapped her foot and huffed out a breath. "Look, it's lunchtime here, too. Deal with it." She jabbed a button and slid the phone back on her belt as she strode across the room. "Sorry I'm late. I thought this was an all-day program."

Rachel rose. "The Club Juniors program runs a full day. Art from the Sea is a special half-day offering."

A flicker of annoyance darkened the woman's eyes. "Too bad someone didn't bother to explain that when I signed Madeleine up. Now I'll have to make other arrangements for the afternoon—and I have to be back at the convention center in half an hour to finish my presentation."

"I can take care of Madeleine for the rest of the day if you'd like." The words spilled out before Rachel could stop them.

The child's mother did a double-take, clearly as surprised by the offer as Rachel was—but she wasted no time accepting. "That would be great. I'm sure you're qualified to work with children or the hotel wouldn't have hired you. Since I've arranged a sitter for my business dinner this evening, I'd only need you to take care of her until six."

"Fine. We'll meet you in the lobby then."

"I'll discuss compensation with you later and reimburse you for any expenses." The woman swiveled around and started for the door.

"I drew a picture, Mommy."

At her daughter's soft comment, the woman looked over her shoulder without slowing her pace. "You can show me later. Be good for the nice lady." She disappeared out the door.

The room went silent.

Rachel caught the slight tremble in Madeleine's lower lip—and had a sudden urge to yank the mother back into the room by her trendy layered hair and give her a piece of her mind. Since that wasn't possible, she'd do the next best thing. She'd put the little girl center stage for the next five and a half hours and lavish her with attention.

Adopting a bright tone, she stood. "Have you been to the Sea Turtle Center yet?"

Madeleine shook her head and rose more slowly, gathering up her watercolor and the art board with the single shell clinging tenuously to the corner.

"Then we'll go there after lunch. It's one of my favorite places on the island."

The little girl didn't respond as she walked over to the trash can in the corner and deposited her half-hearted attempts at art.

Rachel had no difficulty interpreting the child's reasoning. Since no one was going to admire or gush over her handiwork, why bother saving it?

Taking her hand, Rachel led her from the room.

All the while wondering why God gave children to women who couldn't care less about being a parent but snatched them away from those who yearned to be mothers.

Chapter Four

Fletch glanced in his rearview mirror, started to back out of the parking lot at the Sea Turtle Center—and jammed on his brake as an attractive blonde came into view.

She was some distance away, at the edge of the lot for the hotel, burdened down with two large tote bags and a shoulder purse as she wove among the cars. Yet he had no trouble identifying her.

Rachel Shaw.

But it was a different Rachel Shaw than the feisty woman he'd encountered on the beach and at Gram's house.

This Rachel's bent head and slumped shoulders communicated weariness—or discouragement…or both. What had happened to dampen her spunky spirit?

He frowned as he continued to follow her progress. He ought to just leave. The mental state of Eleanor's niece was no concern of his.

Yet for some reason her dejected posture bothered him.

Fletch drummed a finger on the wheel as Gram's admonition about manners echoed in his ears.

Polish them up. You were raised better than that.

He blocked out the part of her comment about attracting a nice girl. His impulse to go to Rachel's aid had nothing to do with creating a more favorable impression on her. But Gram was right. He *had* been raised better than to let a woman carry heavy stuff without assistance. The influence of his Southern upbringing might have faded through the years, but enough remained to niggle at his conscience as he watched his beach companion from last week trudge along—especially after her purse slipped and she almost lost her grip on one of the tote bags.

With a quick shift of gears, Fletch pulled back into his spot, slid out of the SUV, and wove toward her through the cars.

Rachel was plodding along, head bowed, when he stopped a few feet in front of her.

"We meet again."

As he parroted her words from Sunday back to her, her chin jerked up and she came to an abrupt halt.

Fletch gestured toward the overstuffed tote bags. "You look like you could use a hand."

Her gaze flicked to his leg.

His temper flared.

What was with her, anyway? She'd seen him

swim, watched him walk without any problem on the deep, shifting sand. If they'd met under any other circumstances she wouldn't know he had a prosthesis. What did he have to do to prove he was fully mobile—dance the tango?

Since that wasn't an option even if he had two good legs, Fletch settled for grabbing both bags from her before she could protest. "Where are you parked?" The question came out more clipped and curt than he intended.

Rachel looked up—and his breath jammed in his lungs.

Her jade eyes shimmered with distress, and that braid thing she did with her hair accentuated the taut planes of her face. When she swallowed and moistened her lips, a twinge of some unidentifiable emotion tugged at his heart.

He cleared his throat—and softened his tone. "Your car?"

Rachel gestured to her right. "The silver Focus." As she spoke, she led the way, giving him an excellent view of sandaled feet with polished toenails, shapely legs outlined by white capris and a trim waist belted with a silky scarf. As for those soft wisps of hair that had escaped her braid…they whispered at the neck of her sleeveless knit top, calling out to be touched.

While she popped the trunk with the remote, he took a deep breath.

Don't go there, Fletcher. Rachel Shaw might be attractive, but you don't need a summertime romance—even if she could get past the leg issue. She's the niece of your grandmother's best friend. This would only complicate your life.

Check.

After setting the bulky bags inside the trunk, Fletch lowered the lid and faced her, searching for some innocuous comment to ease the tension that seemed to underscore their every encounter. "Must have been quite a shopping trip—though your frown would suggest it wasn't successful."

She positioned her purse in front of her and gripped it like a shield. "The Pier Road shops are more for tourists. Besides, I'm not a shopper."

That was one thing in her favor, at least. How some women could roam through malls for hours with no agenda was mind-boggling. If you were going to a store, you made a list, bought what you needed and left. Anything else was a waste of time.

When the silence lengthened and Rachel didn't pick up on his subtle offer to share what was bothering her, Fletch took the cue and stepped back. "Enjoy the rest of your evening."

He expected her to return the sentiment and make a beeline for the driver's seat.

Instead, she stayed where she was and caught her lower lip between her teeth. "Look…I'm sorry."

At her off-script comment, he frowned. "For what?"

"I stared at your leg again." Bright spots of color appeared on her cheeks, but she didn't break eye contact. "The truth is, I've never met anyone with an artificial limb. I always assumed it would be a major impediment, but you swim better than anyone I've ever met—and you have absolutely no limp. I'm awestruck...and totally impressed. But staring is rude, and I understand why you'd be offended. So I apologize."

He appraised her in silence. Was her explanation on the level?

Maybe.

The sincerity and contrition in her eyes seemed legit. There wasn't a shred of deceit—or pity—in her expression.

Meaning he'd overreacted. Big-time.

Fletch relaxed his posture and summoned up a smile. "Apology accepted. Let's just say we got off on the wrong foot and start over—pun intended."

Her eyes widened, as if she hadn't expected him to find any humor in the situation, and then her own lips wobbled up. "Thanks for being a good sport about it."

"It's either that or go through life feeling sorry for myself. So what brought you to the historic area today?"

Rachel's tremulous smile faded. "I teach a children's art class at the hotel two days a week every summer. Today was my first session of the season."

"It didn't go well?"

"Most of the kids had a great time. But there was one little girl…" Her voice trailed off and she gave him an apologetic shrug. "I'm sure you have better things to do than listen to my tale of woe."

Yeah, he did. Newark was expecting an answer to a lengthy email, and he had some schematics to review for a new military aircraft manufacturing facility in Washington state. He also had to prep for a wee-hours-of-the-morning conference call with one of his European clients.

But as the dipping sun gilded Rachel's hair and she looked up at him with those vivid green eyes, work was suddenly the furthest thing from his mind.

"To be honest, I'm at loose ends for a couple of hours. I dropped Gram off at the Sea Turtle Center for some special event she's helping with, and I was going to grab a quick dinner. Have you eaten yet?"

"No."

"I'll tell you what. If you keep me company during dinner, I'll listen to your tale."

As the words hung in the air between them, Fletch frowned. Where in the world had that come from?

Rachel seemed clueless, too. She gave him a wary look and played with the strap of her purse. "Aunt El had a meeting at church, but she was going to leave me a plate in the fridge."

There's your out, Fletch. Take it.

But once again, foolish words slipped out.

"Eat it for lunch tomorrow."

What was going on here?

Before he had a chance to ponder that question, Rachel did that distracting lip-moistening thing again, drawing his attention to the soft curve of her mouth. The woman had great lips. Lush and full and very kissable…

"Okay."

He jerked his gaze back to her eyes. "What?"

"I said I'd have dinner with you."

Dinner. Right.

Fletch did his best to keep the heat on his neck from creeping above the collar of his sport shirt. "Great. Any recommendations? Everything was shut down when I came at Christmas, and I've only been here for a few days this trip."

"Fins is pleasant. It's on the other side of the island, but Shell Road cuts straight through. It has a deck that overlooks the beach, if you like to eat outside."

"Works for me. I'll follow you." Fletch gestured across the parking lot. "I'm in the black Explorer."

Rachel eyed it. "That looks very tactical—which seems appropriate for a former Navy SEAL."

He folded his arms. "You know my background?"

"Only a few basics. Aunt El's been dropping crumbs since Sunday. In case you haven't figured it out, it was no accident we were both on that otherwise empty beach."

"I figured it out." But Gram had been far less forthcoming with information about the woman standing in front of him. It was hard to blame her, though, given his clear back-off messages. "What else did she tell you?"

Rachel lifted one shoulder. "Very little. I didn't encourage her for fear I'd send the wrong message."

"Which would be…?"

Her cheeks pinkened again, but she didn't shy away from the question. "Aunt El's decided I need some romance in my life, even though I've told her I'm not in the market. I have a feeling she'll latch on to anyone I show the remotest interest in—especially if that person is someone she's already decided might be suitable. So I've been playing down our meeting. All I know is that you lost your leg in the Middle East, you live in Norfolk and you're involved in some kind of security work."

"I know less about you. It seems I have some catching up to do." Like finding out what had happened to her husband. He couldn't ask Gram for the same reason Rachel couldn't ask Eleanor about him, but maybe the woman herself would tell him.

She shifted and tightened her grip on her purse, her taut posture suggesting otherwise. "I lead a very quiet existence as a grade-school art teacher in Richmond. You'll fall asleep in your seafood chowder if I tell you my life story. But I wouldn't mind talking through what happened today, if you're still willing to listen. It's been eating at me for hours."

Her message came through loud and clear: personal stuff wasn't on the dinner menu.

And he couldn't fault her caution. They were both here for brief stays. Their homes were in cities a hundred miles apart—not exactly convenient commuting distance. She was "geographically undesirable for dating," as one of his buddies used to put it. Rachel, by her own admission, wasn't interested in romance. The odds were against them even without throwing his own issues into the mix.

Yet he wanted to know more about her—out of curiosity, nothing more. And if he listened to whatever was on her mind about today, maybe she'd open up a little about the rest of her life.

"I'm still willing." He circled her car, and she sent him a surprised look when he pulled the driver's door open. "Gram reprimanded me for my lack of manners on Sunday. I feel compelled to prove I remember a few of the etiquette lessons she drummed into me in my youth."

Without a word, Rachel slid into the car.

"See you in a few minutes." He shut the door, worked his way back to his car…and found himself looking forward to sharing dinner with the lovely blonde.

Strange.

Much as he'd been annoyed at Gram's and Eleanor's orchestration of Sunday's beach encounter, he suddenly wished he'd met Rachel Shaw under dif-

ferent circumstances—and that she wasn't so averse
to considering a new relationship.

Why in the world had she agreed to have dinner
with Louise's grandson—especially after he'd hinted
he'd like to know more about her background?

Rachel guided her Focus along Shell Road, under
the canopy of Spanish moss that clung to the tower-
ing live oaks, past the hotel's golf course, alongside
a family of bicyclists on a carefree holiday.

That was the kind of holiday she'd expected to
have.

Instead, she was dealing with a well-meaning but
misguided aunt who'd decided it was time for her to
reenter the social scene, a forlorn little girl who was
in desperate need of some TLC, and the tall, dark-
haired man close on her tail whose sharp, insightful
eyes told her he wouldn't hesitate to introduce subjects she didn't want to discuss and ask questions she
didn't want to answer.

Maybe she could just order a soft drink and an ap-
petizer and make a quick exit—even if leaving him
in the lurch to finish his dinner alone wasn't the most
polite thing she'd ever done.

But it would be safer. She knew that intuitively…
and she trusted her instincts.

Settled on that strategy, Rachel pulled into a parking place, locked up and waited at the back of her car
as Fletch angled in beside her.

As soon as he joined her, she started toward the restaurant. But at a touch on her arm, she stopped and turned.

"You know, it occurred to me during the drive here that we've never been officially introduced. I think Gram assumed we'd exchanged names on the beach." He extended his hand. "Jack Fletcher. Fletch to my friends."

She regarded his lean fingers. The mere thought of touching him set off a warning bell in her mind, but what choice did she have?

"Rachel Shaw."

His fingers closed over hers—firm, strong and confident. It was the sort of handshake her father always referred to as a "John Wayne grip." The kind that said *I'm here, I'm wearing my white hat and everything's going to be all right.*

So why did she sense danger?

Taking a shaky breath, she tugged her hand free. "Nice to meet you."

"Likewise." He gestured toward the restaurant. "Shall we?"

Without waiting for her to respond, he took her elbow and guided her up the slanting concrete walkway that led to the patio. It was a polite gesture, nothing more; the kind of thing some men did without thinking about it.

But it had been years since anyone had touched her that way.

And despite what she'd told Aunt El about not being in the market for romance, it felt good.

Her lips settled into a firm line. A reaction like that was all the more reason to end this evening as soon as possible. She carried enough guilt already about Mark. The least she could do was be loyal to him for another year or two. She owed him that.

Because if she'd been more attentive, he might still be alive.

Heart suddenly heavy, Rachel let Fletch lead her in silence as the hostess showed them to one of the umbrella-topped tables on the deck that offered a view of the beach beyond the dunes.

Fletch held her chair as she sat, then took the one at a right angle to her. "My compliments on your choice of restaurant. If the food is half as good as the view, this might become a regular stop for me."

"I've never had a bad meal here." She gave the menu a perfunctory scan and set it aside.

"A woman who knows what she wants." Fletch picked up his own menu and smiled at her.

She found herself staring at the killer dimple that appeared in his cheek. How come she hadn't noticed it before?

Then again, they hadn't done a lot of smiling at each other up until now.

"Rachel?"

She tore her gaze from the dimple. "What?"

"I asked if you have any recommendations."

"Oh." She settled her napkin on her lap and dug around in her purse for her sunglasses. "You can't go wrong with the catch of the day."

"Sold."

Fletch closed his menu as she slipped the glasses over her nose and hid behind the dark lenses. She would *not* be caught staring at that dimple—or anything else—again.

For a moment, she thought he was going to comment on her transparent strategy. But he let it pass as the waitress arrived to take their orders.

Fletch deferred to her.

"A Coke and shrimp cocktail."

"And for your entrée?" The woman waited, pencil poised.

"That's all I'm having."

He cocked his head. "I thought this was a dinner."

"I'm a light eater." True enough—though not that light.

He hesitated, as if he suspected that, then chose the grilled grouper special.

After the waitress departed, he leaned back and studied her. Lucky thing she'd put on the glasses now that he was giving her the full treatment with those probing dark eyes.

"The deal was for dinner, not appetizers."

Rachel resisted the urge to squirm. "I might order more later—but if you'd rather call the whole thing off, that's fine."

"No. I intend to stick to my part of the bargain."

Even if you don't.

The unspoken comment hung in the air between them.

The waitress returned with their drinks, buying her a few seconds to come up with a reply.

"I didn't say I was going to leave before you finish."

Based on the skeptical look he gave her, however, she got the distinct feeling he knew that had been her intention.

Thankfully, he didn't pursue the topic.

Instead, he took a long drink of his Coke, leaned forward and clasped his hands on the table. "So tell me what happened today."

His full attention was fixed on her, and she had the oddest feeling he'd tuned everything else out, that nothing existed in his world at this moment except her. Had he learned to summon up that kind of intense focus as a SEAL, or was it a natural ability?

But it didn't matter. She needed to talk through her day, and he was willing to listen. Better to share her concerns with him than with Aunt El, who had enough on her mind already with the problem-plagued church project. Why add to her worries with the story of a neglected little girl?

Rachel took a sip of soda, laced her fingers, and told him about her morning with Madeleine and her subsequent impromptu babysitting gig.

As her shrimp cocktail and his salad were delivered, grooves dented his brow. "I can't believe a mother would forget her own child—or let her child go off with someone she didn't know."

"I can't, either. Yes, I was screened by the hotel, but I'm still a stranger." Rachel picked up one of the shrimps and dipped it in the container of sauce, glad she'd ordered lightly. Thinking about the poor little girl chased away her appetite.

"Did you find out anything else about her situation during the afternoon?"

"Yes. Madeleine perked up quite a bit, and by the end of the day she'd turned into a talking machine. Her parents are separated, and she only sees her dad every other weekend—when he's not out of the country on business. She wasn't certain what her mom's job is except that it involves a lot of meetings, so I asked the mother a few questions when I dropped her off. She's a sales rep for a software developer and spends a lot of time on the road making product pitches and doing demos at corporate meetings. Since she doesn't have any family available to watch Madeleine at home, she drags her along on the trips. I don't know what she'll do in the fall, when it's time for Madeleine to start first grade."

"That's not much of a life for a little girl." Although he'd been eating steadily as he listened to her story, his focus had been on her, not the food.

Rachel nibbled on another shrimp. "No. And I

can't get the image of her sad eyes out of my mind. She's in desperate need of nurturing. She responded to my attention like a parched flower to water, but I was a momentary diversion. She needs what I gave her today on a full-time basis, and it's tearing me up that I can't do a thing to help her." Her voice choked, and she fumbled for her glass of water.

Silence fell between them while she took a drink and tried to compose herself. After all, what could Fletch say? A situation like this held no easy answers, no quick fixes. He was probably sorry now he'd invited her to dinner instead of spending a quiet evening walking the beach or catching up on email. Either would have been far more relaxing than listening to her vent.

Just as she was about to make her excuses and bolt, Fletch pushed aside his salad plate, reached over and covered her clenched fingers with his.

As the warmth of his hand chased some of the chill from her heart, her pulse ticked up.

"You know, when I was eight my four-year-old brother came down with acute bacterial meningitis." Rachel tried to keep breathing, to focus on his words rather than the pressure of his fingers on hers. "His brain swelled, and he began having seizures. It was touch and go for days, and everyone was afraid he'd suffered permanent neurological damage. We'd just moved to Guam, where my dad was stationed at the navy base, but he was at sea when Paul got sick. Mom practically lived at the hospital, and I was passed around from family to family on the base. Everyone was kind, but they were all busy with their own lives. No one had a lot of time for me—except one young wife."

Fletch stopped to take a drink of soda, and Rachel held her breath, hoping he wouldn't retract his hand.

He didn't.

"Long story short, I only saw Susan Forester twice in my life. Her husband was reassigned not long after Paul's health crisis. But I never forgot her. We baked cookies together. Played with her dog. Watched a funny movie. For a few hours with her, I had a normal life. It reminded me there were people out there who did care, and that things could get better. It gave me hope." He let a beat of silence pass. "The point is, brief encounters can have an impact that lasts a lifetime."

Pressure built in Rachel's throat, behind her eyes. Fletch might have said a lot of things in response to her story, but it was almost as if he'd looked into her heart and cherry-picked the perfect words.

"Thank you."

At her soft reply, he stroked his thumb over the back of her hand. "I learned long ago that I couldn't rid the world of all the bad stuff…or even make everything right for the people closest to me." A flash of pain echoed in his eyes, so fast she wouldn't have noticed it if her attention hadn't been riveted on him.

"But small acts of kindness can make a lasting difference. You did the best you could in the short time you had with Madeleine."

"Again—thank you. That does help…even though I still wish I could do more."

"I know the feeling." Fletch removed his hand from hers while the waitress set his meal in front of him, and from the tinge of regret in his tone she had a feeling he wasn't thinking about Madeleine anymore.

Jack Fletcher had some secrets he wasn't sharing—just as she did.

Best to move to safer territory.

She picked up another shrimp and swirled it in the sauce. "What happened to your brother?"

Fletch dug into his grouper. "I'm happy to report he made a full recovery. He's now an executive with a start-up tech firm in Silicon Valley." While he ate, he sang his brother's praises, making no attempt to hide his pride as he concluded. "Paul's smart as a whip and more successful at thirty-one than I'll ever be."

So Fletch was thirty-five.

She tucked that piece of information away.

As for his brother being smarter—she suspected the former Navy SEAL was shortchanging himself.

"I'm glad your story had a happy ending." Rachel swallowed. "I wish they all did."

His fork paused for a tiny fraction as he scooped up some rice, his response confined to a single word. "Yeah."

But in that one syllable she heard a world of hurt that told her some stories in his life hadn't turned out as well. Was he thinking of his missing leg—or were there other chapters he'd rather forget, too?

"Speaking of unhappy endings...Gram told me you're a widow. I'm sorry."

Rachel stiffened. That wasn't a topic she wanted to discuss. "Thanks."

"Was it an accident?"

Her fingers crumpled the napkin in her lap. For a man who'd been so insightful about her feelings toward Madeleine, he was sure missing her cues about this subject.

"No." She chewed the last bite of her shrimp, washed it down with a long gulp of water and reached for her purse.

The gentle touch of Fletch's hand on her arm stopped her. "I'm sorry. I didn't realize that was such a sensitive subject."

She surveyed his plate. Only a few bites remained. "I just don't talk about it much. Since you're almost finished, would you mind if I head home?"

After a beat of silence, he withdrew his hand. "Of course not. I'll walk you to your car."

"That's not necessary." She dug through her purse for her wallet.

"Gram would disagree." He flashed her a grin. "And dinner's on me." He signaled to the waitress and handed over his credit card.

She continued to paw through her oversize shoulder bag. "I want to pay for my own food."

"Rachel."

She looked up.

"The shrimp cocktail and Coke aren't going to break my budget. Besides, I invited you."

"And I bent your ear about Madeleine. I should pay for *your* dinner."

"Next time."

She opened her mouth to continue protesting— then closed it as his comment registered.

Next time?

No way. Not a smart idea. Being with Fletch was way too unsettling, and she'd come to Jekyll Island to be soothed, not stressed.

Silence fell between them until the waitress reappeared with the charge slip. He signed it and rose.

Rachel gestured toward his plate. "You're not finished."

"Close enough. Shall we?"

Without waiting for a response, he took her arm and guided her through the tables. Everyone they passed was laughing, chatting, enjoying the beautiful evening. No one seemed aware of the powerful sparks of electricity that were making her heart misbehave and short-circuiting her lungs.

All of it generated by a simple touch.

This was not good.

Rachel walked faster.

Only when they reached her car and he broke contact did her pulse begin to moderate. "Thank you for dinner—and for listening to my tale about Madeleine."

"Anytime."

What did that mean?

Was he angling for another get-together?

It was hard to tell from his expression. But if so, he was out of luck. There was not going to be an encore of tonight.

Fletch rested his hand on top of her door. "Try not to worry about her too much."

Rachel tossed her purse onto the passenger seat. "Easier said than done. But I guess I'll just have to put it in God's hands."

Silence met that comment, and she swiveled back toward him. Faint creases etched his forehead, and he stuck his hands in his pockets.

Hmm. He'd passed on services Sunday, and the mention of God made him uncomfortable. Her dinner companion was obviously not a churchgoing man.

That was yet another reason to ignore the unwanted spark between them. If she ever felt ready to date again, she'd choose a man of faith. Marriage held enough challenges without adding religious differences to the mix.

Rachel slid into the driver's seat and looked up at him, striving to end the evening on a lighter note. "I'd say 'Drive safe,' but there's not much need to worry about more than a fender bender on Jekyll Island."

A slight flex of the lips was the closest he got to a smile. "It's not Norfolk, that's for sure. See you around."

With that he closed the door.

Taking the cue, she started her car.

Fletch remained where he was while she backed out and drove toward the exit. Only after she pulled onto the ring road did he move toward his SUV. A few seconds later she lost sight of him.

Settling behind the wheel, Rachel flexed her fingers and accelerated. Out of sight, out of mind, right?

If only.

Chapter Five

W hat the…?

Fletch froze in the doorway of the church conference room as six smiling faces turned his way and applause broke out all around.

He looked to Gram for guidance, but she was grinning and clapping along with everyone else.

All at once, the pieces fell into place.

Gram's request that he pick her up from the vacation-house meeting had been a ruse. The committee hadn't assembled to discuss his offer; they'd already decided to accept it and wanted to say thanks.

Warmth crept up his neck.

A note in the mail, or a phone call, would have sufficed.

He shifted from one foot to the other, eyeing the exit down the hall.

Before he could bolt, Gram hurried over to him, linked her arm with his and tugged him into the room.

"Let me introduce my grandson, Jack Fletcher—better known as Fletch. Thanks to him, Francis House is back on track." As the applause resumed, she leaned close. "Don't you just love that name? We decided on it this morning, in honor of Francis of Assisi. He was such a kind, gentle man. We're going to put his peace prayer right in the foyer."

As the applause died down again, a middle-aged man in a clerical collar joined them and extended his hand. "Jim Carlson. I'm the pastor here, and I'm delighted to meet you."

Fletch returned the man's firm shake and mumbled a response.

"Eleanor made her famous coffee cake in your honor." He gestured toward a side table, where the cake, a large urn of coffee and a bowl of fresh fruit waited. "But before we dive in, would you join our meeting for a few minutes?"

Fletch hesitated. What was this all about? The amount he'd offered should be more than sufficient to cover the basic finishing work that was required, and he didn't need any more accolades.

When he sent Gram a questioning look, she busied herself with some papers in front of her rather than meet his gaze.

A niggle of unease raced down his spine. Something was up.

"Fletch?"

At the minister's prompt, he cast one more longing glance toward the door, quashing the urge to make a run for it.

He was stuck.

With a resigned sigh, he followed the man to the empty seat at the table.

"Eleanor, you have the floor." Reverend Carlson reclaimed his chair as Fletch sat.

His grandmother's friend stood and gave him a megawatt smile. "First of all, on behalf of the entire Francis House committee and the congregation as a whole, thank you so much for your generous offer."

He fidgeted, trying without success to find a more comfortable position. "It's no big deal."

"On the contrary. It's a huge deal—especially to the families who will now be able to take their much-needed vacations. The committee's been back and forth on the phone a dozen times since Louise called me yesterday with the news. You're truly the answer to our prayers."

Fletch squirmed again. "I'm glad to help." Then he sent Gram a *Get me out of here!* look.

She ignored him as Eleanor continued. "Now, here's the thing. This project wasn't just supposed to be about monetary donations. It was also intended to be a labor of love. However, as you know, some of our most skilled members have had to renege on their commitments for various reasons. But after a lot of calling around yesterday, we've lined up some reinforcements who've agreed to do a lot of the grunt work. Even Reverend Carlson is going to roll up his sleeves."

The minister held up a hand in warning. "Just be sure to assign me to some task where I can't do any damage—and nothing pipe-related. The last time I picked up a wrench at home we ended up with a several-hundred-dollar plumbing bill."

"Duly noted," Eleanor said. "In fact, we'll bring in the experts for the remaining plumbing and electrical work. So Fletch, we'd like to accept your offer of a donation in an amount that will cover those repairs. We've got some estimates here…" She riffled through the papers in front of her and passed a couple of them around the table in his direction. "If you could cover those items, we'd be grateful."

When the estimates reached him, Fletch gave them a quick scan and did some mental math. The total was far less than the amount he'd offered to Gram after she'd asked him for a ballpark figure on his contribution.

"Are you certain this is all you need?"

"Yes. As I said, we've lined up additional members of the congregation to give us some hands-on assistance. Even Louise and I are going to pitch in."

Fletch frowned at Gram. "You have a broken wrist."

His grandmother sat up straighter. "I may be having trouble with zippers and lids, and I might not be able to drive, but I'm not useless. I'm sure the crew can find simple jobs for me to do. I don't need two hands to scrub a stovetop or hold a ladder while someone paints."

Gram holding a ladder with one wrist in a cast while some amateur was painting above her.

That recipe for disaster sent a chill down his spine.

Before he could voice his concerns, Eleanor stepped back in. "We'll all be careful, Fletch. With these old bones, none of us can afford to take any chances. I'll watch out for Louise. And maybe we'll round up enough volunteers to keep her on the sidelines." She sent him a pointed look. "Of course, we wouldn't turn down an offer of assistance from an able-bodied younger man."

A beat of silence ticked by as six pairs of eyes swiveled toward him.

"Now, Eleanor." Gram turned to her partner in crime. "Fletch is a busy man. He's not here on vacation."

"I realize that. I just thought he might be able to spare an evening or two for some painting or sanding or some such thing. He'd probably get more done in an hour than most of our volunteers would accomplish in three, seeing how slowly some of them move. I wanted to give him an opportunity to contribute in a more concrete way, that's all."

If Gram was in on this manipulation caper, you'd never know it from her innocent expression.

But Fletch wasn't writing off the possibility. Nor did he intend to be conned into a home-repair gig.

He was about to make his excuses when Reverend Carlson spoke.

"We don't want to put you under any pressure, Fletch. You're already being more than generous with your financial donation. If you can't spare two or three hours a week, we understand."

Two or three hours a week.

His stomach bottomed out.

No one was too busy to give that amount of time, especially for a worthwhile cause—and every person at the table knew it.

Fletch let out a slow breath, feeling as he had the day his ten-year-old buddy Justin Hoff had suckered him into taking care of his vegetable plot while the family went on vacation for two weeks. "It'll be easy," Justin had said. "Just water it with the hose every other day and pull a few weeds."

Ha.

Fletch had ended up waging a battle against an army of rabbits intent on decimating the lettuce patch. Hauled bucket after bucket of water across the street several times a day when the Hoffs' hose burst and the temperature soared during a record-breaking heat wave. Blistered his hands pulling the rampant weeds that thrived in the scorching weather even as the vegetables withered.

And in the end, what had he had to show for his efforts?

A miffed friend who thought he'd fallen down on

the job, a painful sunburn and a lingering feeling he'd been had.

His gut told him this project could leave him with the same feeling.

Yet as he gazed at the Good Samaritans around the table and thought about the problem-plagued families in the file he'd skimmed, he couldn't say no.

"I think I can spare a few hours here and there."

"Wonderful!" Eleanor sent him another dazzling smile, tapped the papers in front of her into a neat pile and stood. "Now let's eat cake."

When he rose, the rest of the good-intentioned group crowded around him, shaking his hand, slapping him on the back, assuring him they would be grateful for any time he could spare.

But as the minister guided him toward the food table, he hoped their good intentions weren't paving a path toward a place he'd prefer to avoid.

"Were you serious yesterday morning, when you offered to help out at Francis House, dear?" Aunt El set a plastic-wrap-covered plate on the kitchen table. "This is supposed to be your vacation."

"Very serious." Rachel lifted the edge of the plastic and pressed her fingers against the crumbs—all that remained of the cinnamon coffee cake her aunt had baked for this morning's meeting at church. "I see your cake was a hit."

"Yes. And the meeting went well, too. It was so

generous of Fletch to make that contribution. Such a nice man, don't you think?"

Rachel captured the last crumb and popped it in her mouth instead of responding.

"Don't you think?" Aunt El prodded.

"Think what?"

"That Fletch is a nice man."

"Seems to be."

Her aunt heaved a sigh and tugged the plate away from her. "I'll add your name to the list of volunteers before I make up the work schedule." She crossed to the sink and deposited the plate. "As for Fletch…"

The phone trilled.

Yes! Perfect timing.

Rachel lunged for it. "I'll get that."

"Help yourself. I need to put this in my bedroom." Eleanor indicated the sweater in her hand. "Reverend Carlson keeps that meeting room like an icebox. Must be his Wisconsin upbringing."

While her aunt moved down the hall, Rachel snagged the phone from the holder and greeted the caller.

"Rachel?"

"Yes."

"This is Mary Richards from guest relations at the Jekyll Island Club Hotel. One of our guests would like to speak with you. A Carolyn Butler."

Madeleine's mother?

Odd.

Rachel picked up the pen from beside the pad of paper by the phone. "If you'll give me her phone number, I'll call her."

The woman recited it. "That's her cell. I just spoke with her, and she sounded quite anxious to reach you."

"I'll call her as soon as we hang up. Thanks for passing on the message."

Once they said their goodbyes, Rachel pressed the switch hook, waited for the dial tone and tapped in the number.

The woman answered on the first ring, an almost palpable distress quivering through her taut hello.

"Ms. Butler? This is Rachel Shaw. I babysat your…"

"Yes, I know who you are. Thank you for calling so quickly. Look…I don't mean to impose, but Madeleine's sick and…" Her voice broke.

Rachel's heart skipped a beat, and she tightened her grip on the phone. "What's wrong with her?"

"They think it might be appendicitis. Here's the thing. She's really scared, and she keeps asking for you." Once again her voice choked. "I know it's a huge imposition, but I wondered if you might be able to come by for a few minutes. We're in the E.R. at the hospital in Brunswick."

"Yes." Rachel didn't hesitate. "I'll get there as fast as I can. Tell Madeleine I'm on my way."

As she said goodbye and dropped the phone back into the cradle, Eleanor returned to the kitchen.

"I made some chicken salad if you'd—" Her aunt came to an abrupt halt. "What's wrong?"

Rachel grabbed her purse and gave her the shorthand version while she groped for her keys.

"My. Madeleine must have been very taken with you."

Only because she was in desperate need of a mother figure—but Rachel left that unsaid. No need for Aunt El to worry about the neglected child, too.

"We spent the whole day together." She started for the door. "I guess she had a lot of fun. I have no idea when I'll be back. Don't wait dinner for me."

"Do you know how to get there?"

Rachel stopped. "No."

"Call me from the outskirts of town and I'll walk you through the directions."

She hesitated, then pushed the door open. "I'll do that. Thanks."

She'd just have to trust that Aunt El was better at phone directions than she was at passing on verbal instructions for her killer coffee cake. Forgetting to mention that the egg whites were supposed to be beaten had led to a dud that was still the butt of jokes in the teachers' lounge.

But half an hour later, as the hospital's E.R. entrance came into sight, it was clear her aunt was more adept at relaying routes than recipes.

"I'm here." Rachel pulled in and inspected the packed lot, searching for an empty spot. Once she homed in on one, she accelerated toward it. "I'll call you when I know…"

Thwump. Thwump. Thwump.

What in the world was that weird noise?

"Rachel? Your phone must have cut out. I missed whatever you just said."

Struggling with the suddenly uncooperative wheel, she pulled into the empty spot.

"Rachel?"

"Yeah, I'm here. Hang on a sec." She set the brake, pushed her door open and slid out with a sinking feeling. She'd heard a noise like that once before, years ago.

Hoping she was wrong, she circled the car.

She wasn't.

Her right front tire was flat as the proverbial pancake.

Expelling a breath, she snagged the phone off the seat, set the locks and started toward the entrance of the hospital. "I'm back, Aunt El. You're never going to believe this. I have a flat tire."

"Oh, for goodness' sake. And there you are on a mission of mercy." She tut-tutted. "Sometimes I have to wonder what the good Lord is thinking."

You and me both.

"It could be worse, I suppose." Rachel picked up

her pace. "Though I have to admit, changing a tire isn't high on my list of favorite activities."

"Now don't you even think about doing such a thing. After living here all these years, I have people lined up for jobs like that. I know just who to call. You go see that little girl and don't spend a minute worrying about that tire."

"You're a life saver." The doors to the E.R. whooshed open and she headed straight for the intake desk.

"Hold that thought. And call me later with an update."

The phone clicked off, and Rachel shoved it in her purse as she approached the window.

"Could you let Carolyn Butler know I'm here? Her daughter, Madeleine, was brought in earlier with a possible case of appendicitis."

The woman consulted the computer screen in front of her. "She's in the surgical waiting room. Let me give you directions."

Surgical waiting room. It must have been appendicitis after all.

Five minutes later, she found Carolyn slumped in a chair in one corner of the sterile room, her head in her hands.

At least the woman wasn't on her cell or laptop, trying to catch up on email while the doctor operated.

A twinge of guilt pricked her conscience.

Not very Christian, Rachel. The woman's obviously distraught. Cut her a little slack.

Doing her best to refrain from judging, Rachel approached Madeleine's mother. "Ms. Butler?"

The woman looked up. It took a second for recognition to dawn in her eyes. "It's Carolyn. And thank you for coming."

"How's Madeleine?"

"In surgery. Her white blood count was off the charts." She closed her eyes, and her features contorted. "I should have listened when she started complaining about a stomachache on Monday night. But I assumed it was just some bug, you know?" The woman looked at her, seeking reassurance.

The one thing Rachel couldn't offer.

Because she'd struggled with plenty of second thoughts herself, gone through the whole "should have" list over and over and over again.

She still did.

Swallowing past the lump in her throat, she took the seat beside Carolyn. "What did the doctors say?"

The woman combed her fingers through her not-so-stylishly mussed hair. "That I shouldn't blame myself. That diagnosing appendicitis in children is tough because they don't have a lot of the typical adult symptoms. That if it ruptures, she could have life-threatening complications." Her face crumpled. "I still feel like such a terrible mother. I never realized how disconnected I'd become from her until she asked for you in the E.R. I was standing right there, and she wanted you."

Rachel remained silent. What could she say in response to the woman's anguished words?

Madeleine's mother didn't seem to expect a reply. Her focus remained on the carpet, the knuckles of her knotted fingers whitening. "The thing is, I've always been career-focused. My husband worked hard, too, but he was better at balancing things. He travelled quite a bit, but when he was home, he was home. You know what I mean?"

Yeah, she did. Mark had been like that, too—a hard worker with rock-solid priorities. God and family had always come first.

He'd have made a wonderful father.

Her stomach kinked, and she gritted her teeth. Now wasn't the time to rehash all that. She needed to put her own regrets aside and focus on the distraught woman beside her.

"Steve tried to get me to see the light, to realize I was missing out on the important stuff in life. But I couldn't dial it down. Eventually I got to the point where I never left work behind. So he left me." Carolyn sniffed. "All because I was s-scared."

Not what Rachel had expected.

"Why were you scared?"

The woman finally looked up, a world of hurt in her eyes. "Because you can't count on other people. When I was ten, my father walked out the door one night and never came back. After watching my mom struggle for years to keep a roof over our heads, I vowed I'd never put myself in that position. So I worked hard. Too hard, I guess. Harder still since Steve left. I have to make sure I can provide for Madeleine, you know?" She swiped at her tears. "Now I have a great job—but my husband's gone and my daughter would rather be comforted by a kind woman she just met than her own mother. I don't even think she loves me anymore."

As Carolyn fished in her purse and withdrew a tissue, Rachel took a long, slow breath.

This was why you shouldn't judge people. Things weren't always as clear-cut as they seemed. Carolyn wasn't a mother more enamored with her job than her child. She was a woman who bore scars and feared rejection. A woman who was running scared and making bad decisions based on the past, not the present.

She was a woman who needed understanding and guidance, not criticism.

"Madeleine does love you." Rachel leaned forward and touched her hand. "And she wants to know you love her, too. If she didn't care anymore, she wouldn't have asked you to look at her artwork yesterday."

A glimmer of something—perhaps hope—flashed in the woman's eyes. Then it dimmed. "But I didn't have time for her."

"You could change that going forward. I'm a

grade-school art teacher, and I've seen remarkable things happen when parents make more time for their children."

"I'd like to think that could happen."

"There's no reason it couldn't."

The woman bit her lower lip. "Except after this, Steve may not give me a second chance. He wanted custody when we separated. He might push harder now."

"Maybe not—if you're willing to make some changes."

As Carolyn's expression grew thoughtful, a man in surgical scrubs appeared in the doorway. "Mrs. Butler?"

Carolyn vaulted to her feet. "Here."

The surgeon crossed the room and joined them. "Let's sit for a minute and I'll bring you up to speed."

Rachel started to rise, but Carolyn waved her back into her seat, making it clear she wanted her to stay.

And as the physician pulled up a chair, Rachel prayed for good news about Madeleine—and for a fresh start for her fractured family.

Chapter Six

He could have called Rachel on her cell—or simply finished the job and walked away. There was no need to make personal contact.

Except he wanted to.

Ignoring the little voice in his head telling him this wasn't the best way to stay uninvolved, Fletch dodged a meal cart and checked the pediatric-floor room numbers along the corridor. It should be the next one.

As he approached, conversation filtered out.

"…and Daddy will arrive soon." An unfamiliar female voice.

A child responded, too softly to discern the words.

"I'm here, honey." Rachel.

"Will you stay?" The little girl again.

"Of course. At least until your daddy gets here."

Fletch paused on the threshold. Given how upset she'd been yesterday, he wasn't surprised Rachel had come running when Madeleine asked for her. But according to Eleanor, she'd been here since noon—almost six hours. And he had a feeling she'd spend the night if the little girl asked.

Funny. Based on their first encounter at the beach, he'd never have guessed she had such a sensitive and compassionate heart.

Just went to show how easy it was to jump to wrong conclusions.

Lifting his hand, he gave one quick knock on the open door and stepped inside.

Three people looked his direction—but his focus was on Rachel, who was holding the young patient's hand.

Her eyes widened, and her lips parted slightly. "What are you doing here?"

He held up the spare car key he'd found secured with a magnet inside her front wheel well—just where Eleanor had said it would be. "Jack's Garage, at your service. Can I talk to you for a minute?" He inclined his head toward the hall and retreated.

Rachel joined him a moment later, frustration etched on her features. "I can't believe Aunt El called you."

"You're welcome."

A faint flush stained her cheeks. "Thank you."

"Wrong order, but I'll take it." Fletch handed over the key and gestured toward the room. "How's she doing?"

"The prognosis is excellent. Thankfully, her appendix didn't rupture." Rachel examined the key, then slid it into the pocket of her capris and exhaled. "Look, I'm sorry Aunt El bothered you. When she told me she'd amassed all kinds of resources for stuff like this during her years on Jekyll and knew just who to call, I didn't have a clue it was you. I apologize for the imposition."

"It wasn't an imposition." That was a stretch. Eleanor had interrupted him in the middle of a complicated schematics review—but he could pick that up again later tonight. He propped one shoulder against the wall and folded his arms, assessing the faint shadows under eyes. "You look tired—and stressed."

She made a face. "Hospitals aren't my favorite place."

"Mine, either."

As Fletch fought back a wave of unpleasant memories, he caught sight of a tall, late-thirtyish man striding down the hall, his tie askew, his face taut with worry. He was heading straight for Madeleine's room. After giving them a distracted glance, he brushed by and entered.

"Madeleine's father, I presume. Why don't we give them a few minutes alone?" He gestured toward the waiting room he'd passed on his way from the elevator.

Rachel hesitated. "You don't need to hang around."

"Trying to get rid of me?"

"No. Trying not to take up any more of your day—and to figure out how to repay you for taking care of my tire."

"No repayment necessary."

"I don't like being in people's debt."

"You only incur debt if you borrow. I donated." He took her arm and guided her down the hall, indicating a soda machine as they entered the waiting room. "Can I get you a drink?"

"Why don't I get you one?" Already she was rummaging through her purse.

Since she seemed set on a concrete thank-you, he relented. "A Sprite sounds good."

After purchasing two sodas, Rachel joined him in the corner and claimed the chair beside him.

He popped the tab on his. "Eleanor gave me the topline. You want to fill in the details?"

While he downed his soda, Rachel recounted the events that had led up to her mad dash to the hospital—as well as what had transpired in the past six hours.

"Sounds like Madeleine's mother has a few issues."

"More than. But I'm praying this was a wake-up call that brings about some positive changes in all their lives—especially Madeleine's." She ran a fingertip down a trail of condensation on the side of the can. "Children are such a precious gift...my heart breaks when people don't realize that and treasure each day with them."

Weighing his can in his hand, Fletch studied her. He already knew she had a tender spot for children. Why be a teacher if you didn't? Or take on extra classes during your summer vacation instead of lazing around on the beach? Plus, her feelings had come through loud and clear last night as she'd shared her angst over Madeleine's situation.

But his gut told him there was a personal component to her last statement—and his gut never lied.

He'd learned that the hard way.

Swigging back the last of the soda, Fletch tried to wash away the lingering bad taste.

It didn't work.

The can crinkled beneath his grip, and he loosened his fingers. "Madeleine's lucky to have found a friend in you."

Rachel shook her head. "It would be better if she bonded with her mother. But maybe that will happen."

"Have you always loved kids?"

"What's not to love?"

"Let's see." Fletch pretended to consider. "Messy diapers, midnight feedings and ear-piercing wails come to mind."

Her expression grew solemn, derailing his attempt at humor. "You don't like children?"

"I didn't say that. But life with kids isn't always rosy. Ask any parent."

Rachel wrapped both hands around her soda can and gave him an appraising look. "That almost sounds as if you're speaking from experience."

Despite a sudden hollow feeling in the pit of his stomach, he managed to conjure up a smile. "As a son, not a parent. I watched my mom and dad contend with two boys. It wasn't always fun and games."

"I bet there were plenty of happy times, too."

"Why do you say that?"

"From what I've seen, you turned out fine—and kids who turn out fine have usually had a solid support system growing up. They also tend to make good parents."

The hollow feeling spread.

Time to put the spotlight back on her.

"Using that same yardstick, you must have had a solid support system, too."

"The best. I still do, even though we're scattered now. My dad's with the State Department, and he and Mom live in Cairo. My brother and his wife live in London."

"It must be tough to orchestrate family get-togethers."

"It is." She swallowed. "The last time we were all together was after my husband died three years ago."

The very subject he'd been curious about—and

she'd introduced it. Last night, however, she'd backed off when he'd probed.

Dare he try again?

Maybe—if he approached with caution.

"I understand that's a sensitive subject, but I have to admit I'm curious about what happened to him." Fletch put as much empathy as possible into his tone, choosing his words with care. "He had to be young."

Several seconds of silence ticked by, and he expected her to change the subject. But she didn't.

"Too young. Thirty-three. He got melanoma. It was stage four before we discovered it. The cancer was in his lymph nodes, and it spread faster than he could be treated…to his liver, lungs, kidneys—every major organ. I watched him go from a healthy bike rider and jogger to a bedridden invalid in just a few weeks." Her voice hoarsened, and she swallowed. "He was dead in three months."

In the silence that followed, Fletch grappled with her news. He thought he'd had problems, but a story like hers restored perspective—fast.

As he tried to come up with some kind of response, Rachel looked over at him. "You don't need to say anything. People always feel as if they have to offer some sort of platitude, but what is there to say beyond 'I'm sorry'? 'It was a tragedy.' 'He was too young.' 'Rely on God.' 'There's a reason for everything.' 'He's in a better place.' 'If there's anything I can do…'" Her shoulders hunched. "But no one can do the one thing that would make it better—bring him back. So I'm left to struggle with the loss and the…" She stopped.

The what?

Before he could ask, Rachel pressed her lips together, stood and eased away. "As long as both of Madeleine's parents are here now, I think I'll say goodbye and head home. Thank you again."

The distance she'd put between them was more than physical, the message clear: *I'm done talking.*

So much for his idea of suggesting they grab a bite before heading back to the island.

He rose, too. "I put your deflated tire in the trunk. A garage can test it for you, see if it's salvageable."

"Thanks. I'll take care of it. See you around."

With that, Rachel fled the waiting room and disappeared down the hall.

Juggling his keys in one hand, Fletch weighed her parting words as he headed toward the elevator. See you around? Not if she could help it. At least that's the distinct impression she'd left.

And that was a good thing, right? Hadn't he come to the same conclusion mere days ago? It was obvious she had baggage. He had a ton of it. There couldn't be much benefit in two people who were dealing with major issues striking up any sort of relationship.

At the elevator, he jabbed the button for the ground

floor. He should be glad she'd stepped back. It would save them both a lot of grief.

So how come he wasn't?

Rachel brushed a wisp of hair back into her French braid, skimmed the directions to Francis House Aunt El had given her and hung a right off Captain Wylly Road. According to her notes, the cottage was a pale yellow one-story, five houses down on the right with a live oak in the...

She jammed on her brakes as the house came into view—along with the black Explorer in the driveway.

Fletch's SUV? He'd volunteered to contribute sweat equity as well as dollars?

Funny how Aunt El had neglected to mention that. Not.

Mouth settling into a straight line, Rachel pulled to the side of the road, dug around in her purse for her cell and punched in her aunt's number.

The phone rang once. Twice. Three times.

Then it rolled to voice mail.

Aunt El was ignoring her. When she'd left less than five minutes ago, her aunt had been settling in on the screened porch with a glass of lemonade and a new romance novel, her portable phone at hand.

This was a setup. What else could it be? Her aunt coordinated the work-crew schedule.

Rachel huffed out a breath. The two of them were going to have to have a long talk later.

But in the meantime, what was she supposed to do? She'd promised to help out, and reneging on a commitment didn't sit well.

Foot still on the brake, she eyed the other car in the driveway. At least she and Fletch wouldn't be alone. That would help keep things businesslike and impersonal.

She hoped.

Resigned, Rachel released the brake and covered the remaining distance, squeezing into the driveway behind the second car, next to Fletch's SUV.

As she walked toward the front door, she smoothed a hand down her ratty khaki shorts and tugged at the hem of the faded Art in the Park T-shirt that had shrunk from too many washings. Aunt El had said to dress cool, since the air conditioner hadn't yet been repaired, and to wear old clothes. This outfit was about as old and cool as it got—and scraped the bottom of the attractive scale.

Then again, why should she care? It wasn't as if she was angling for a date or anything.

Straightening her shoulders, Rachel marched up to the open front door, gave a cursory knock and called out as she crossed the threshold. "New volunteer reporting for duty."

A clatter sounded from somewhere in the recesses of the house, to her left.

Five seconds later, a wiry, white-haired man holding a hammer appeared from the doorway to the right. "You must be Rachel. I'm Hank Adams, the so-called shift leader of our motley crew. Big title, no authority. The story of my life." He gave her a jaunty salute and extended his hand. "Welcome."

She returned his firm shake, liking the merry twinkle in his clear, blue eyes. "Nice to meet you."

"I see you came dressed to work." He gave her a quick sweep. "Excellent. Remodeling is a messy business. So…tonight you have the option of painting a bedroom or cleaning grout in the bathroom. What a choice, huh?"

The man's good humor was infectious, despite the oppressive heat in the stuffy house.

"I think I'll go with the painting."

"Can't say I blame you. Our other volunteer is also on paint duty, so I'll turn you over to him and he can show you the ropes." The man started down the hall.

Rachel held back.

Was it too late to opt for the grout detail?

But Hank had already disappeared.

Besides, what excuse would she use? *I don't want to work alongside Fletch because he makes me nervous? Because he stirs up emotions I'm not ready to feel? Because when I'm with him, I forget about Mark—which only adds to my guilt?*

As if she could say any of that.

She'd have to suck it up and deal with the proximity for tonight.

Both men were waiting by the time she reached

the last room at the end of the hall. Well, Hank was waiting. Fletch was picking up a bunch of supplies that must have been in the overturned bucket on the floor. The one he'd knocked over, perhaps, after she'd called out to announce her arrival—because he'd been as surprised as she was?

"So…as you can see, we're painting this children's bedroom yellow. We'll have bunk beds over there," Hank motioned to the right, then to the left, "and a chest of drawers over there." He propped his hands on his hips and looked down as Fletch retrieved the last runaway roll of painter's tape. "Close call. If that had been a can of paint, we'd have had a real mess on our hands."

"Yeah." Fletch tossed the tape back in the bucket and angled away to stretch for a screwdriver, his prosthesis on full display below his cut-off denim shorts.

Thank goodness he was facing the other direction or he'd have found her gawking at his leg again. This prosthesis was nothing like the one he'd worn on the beach. That leg had been crafted to appear lifelike. Today, above his sport shoe, there was just a tube of metal attached to a hard, flesh-colored-shell that fit over the stump of his real leg.

After tossing the screwdriver into the bucket, Fletch stood and turned toward her. "Hello, Rachel."

"Hi." She kept her gaze on his face.

Hank looked from one to the other. "You two know each other?"

"Yeah." Fletch didn't offer more.

"Perfect. That should make being painting partners easier."

Fat chance.

"I'll leave you in Fletch's hands, Rachel." Beats of charged silence pulsed in the room as Fletch gave her a swift but thorough scan.

Resisting the urge to tug on the hem of her shorts, she edged closer to the oscillating fan in the corner. Maybe it would cool her down a few degrees. "So how can I help?"

Fletch indicated the baseboards and crown molding. "That's supposed to be white. You could tackle the trim on the walls I've finished—unless you'd rather help me roll over there." He tipped his head toward a half-painted wall.

Work within touching distance of the tall ex-SEAL, or paint in the opposite corner of the room, as far as possible from him.

One option was appealing.

The other was safe.

She went with safe.

"Detail work is my strong suit. I'll take the trim." She started toward the can of white paint.

"You want me to open it for you?"

"I can handle it. I've done my share of remodeling work." She reached for the can of paint and the opener. "Mark and I bought a fixer-upper a couple of years before he died."

For an instant she froze.

Why had those words come out so easily? She never talked about her life with Mark.

And when had the sharp pain that seared through her whenever she mentioned him subsided to a dull ache?

Since you met the man standing ten feet away.

The answer echoed in her mind, impossible to refute. For whatever reason, in Fletch's presence the past receded. Even the guilt seemed to ebb.

Maybe that was why, try as she might, she couldn't get too angry at Aunt El for setting her up tonight.

But how did Fletch feel about yet another attempt to push them together?

Rachel risked a peek at him as she pried the lid off the can. He was pouring some more paint into the roller pan attached to the ladder. But all at once, as if sensing her scrutiny, he looked her way.

Her first instinct was to break contact with those dark, discerning eyes. To ignore the sudden zip of electricity that buzzed through her nerve endings. Except that was juvenile. They should just deal with any…stuff…that came up between them. Why not be honest? Act like the adults they were?

Taking a deep breath, she curled her fingers around the handle of the paint can. Tight. "It appears we've been set up again."

"You didn't know about this, either?"

"Do you think I'd be here if I did?"

"Why wouldn't you be?"

Good question.

And honesty only went so far.

This time she shifted away and made a project out of selecting one of the brushes from among the choices on the tarp. "It feels awkward. We're both too old for all this matchmaking stuff. Besides, I don't think either of us is interested."

Fletch didn't dispute her statement or drop even the slightest hint that while she might not be interested, he was.

A surge of disappointment swept over her, and she exhaled. How dumb was that? Ten days ago, Jack Fletcher hadn't even been in her life—and she had more important things to do than get involved in a summer romance. That was for teenagers.

Behind her, the aluminum ladder squeaked and she risked another peek at him. He'd gone back to painting the wall with steady, measured strokes, turning the dingy gray walls a bright yellow that brought sunshine into the room.

Kind of like she wished someone would do to her life.

But that, too, was a teenage fantasy. The stuff of fairy tales.

Because as she'd learned, love came with a price. Loss was part of life. And happy endings only happened in storybooks.

Chapter Seven

"My word. You two are going to put the rest of us to shame." Hank stuck his head into the bedroom and gave it a once-over. "You're almost finished with the first coat on the walls *and* the woodwork."

Fletch set the roller in the pan at his feet and checked on Rachel. She was two rungs up the ladder, lines of concentration etched on her forehead as she carefully drew her brush along the edge of the crown molding, trying not to deposit any white paint on the fresh yellow walls.

As she stretched to continue the line, she adopted a ballerina-like pose, leaning forward and extending one long, shapely leg behind her.

Blood pressure spiking, Fletch forced himself to turn back to Hank. Considering how distracted he'd gotten every time he'd looked her way, it was a wonder he'd made any progress at all in the two hours since her arrival.

"It's coming along." Fletch flexed his shoulders to work out the kinks. "How are you doing with the kitchen cabinets?"

"All resecured. I'll tell you, the older gent who owned this house was lucky he didn't meet his maker a lot sooner. A couple of them were ready to fall." Hank stifled a yawn and offered a sheepish grin. "I don't know about you young folks, but I'm ready to call it a night."

Rachel finally joined the conversation. "I've only got a little more to go." She gestured to a six-foot section of dingy crown molding. "I'd rather finish up."

"I don't have much left, either." Fletch surveyed the quarter of a wall remaining. "Might as well knock it out."

"Fine by me. Let me show you how to lock up." Hank looked up at the female half of his painting duo. "Good night, Rachel. Thanks for your help."

"Glad to assist. Nice to meet you, Hank."

As Fletch followed the man down the hall, Hank spoke over his shoulder. "That pretty little lady sure is a hard worker."

"Yes, she is."

"You two make a nice team."

Fletch let that pass.

The man detoured into the kitchen to retrieve his cooler. "You want some more soda before I haul this thing home? It's a hot one tonight."

"Not a bad idea." After the man flipped open the

lid, Fletch pulled two out, juggling the sweaty cans as they continued to the front door and Hank explained the lock.

"Now you go ahead and take that soda back to your helper. I expect you're both parched." Hank shifted the cooler to his other hand. "Will I see you on Tuesday?"

That had been the plan. He'd committed to two nights a week.

What about Rachel? Was she on the same schedule? If so, would she show up again to work with him?

Based on how quiet she'd been tonight, he wasn't counting on it.

Hank squinted at him. "Don't tell me we scared you off already."

"Nope. I'll be back."

"Glad to hear it. With so many people pitching in, I think we might just get this baby done in time for the Mitchell family. I'd sure hate to cancel anyone else's vacation." He pushed through the screen door and called over his shoulder, "See you next week."

Once the door closed behind him, absolute quiet descended in the house. At least while their crew chief had been there, banging and drilling noises had balanced the silence in the bedroom. Now, as Fletch rejoined Rachel, the stillness seemed more pronounced.

He crossed to the ladder. Her back was to him as

she continued to paint, and he held up a can of soda. "Can I tempt you?"

She jerked toward him, teetering.

Whoops. Bad choice of words.

A Freudian slip, perhaps?

Shoving one of the cans under his arm, Fletch grabbed her elbow and held tight until she regained her balance.

"Sorry. I didn't mean to startle you."

As her gaze locked with his, three things registered in rapid succession.

The pulse beating frantically in the hollow of her throat.

The jolt of electricity that made the steamy room even hotter.

The sudden yearning in her eyes that spiked his adrenaline and sent a clear message.

She was, indeed, tempted.

By more than his offer of soda.

Her breath hitched, and she tugged her elbow free. "Thanks." The word rasped, and she broke eye contact. "I could use a cold drink."

So could he.

But standing in front of a supercharged air conditioner would be better.

In silence, Fletch handed over the soda.

Rachel fumbled with the tab, the sudden fizz alleviating the pressure in the can.

Too bad there wasn't some way to alleviate the

thrum of electricity still pinging through the warm air in the suddenly too-small room.

As she lifted the can and took a long swallow, revealing the graceful curve of her throat, Fletch forced himself to back away. Otherwise, he might do something he'd regret.

Maybe staying to finish up hadn't been such a great idea after all.

There was no way out now, though, except to get the job done ASAP and make a fast exit.

He popped the top on his own soda, emptied the can in several long gulps and went back to work, using every mental trick in his repertoire to keep his mind focused on the job.

Fifteen minutes later, when he finished the last swipe with the roller, Rachel was wrapping up, too.

"I'll close up the paint cans if you want to clean the pan and brushes." She busied herself gathering rags as she spoke, keeping her face averted.

In silence, Fletch hauled the items to the kitchen sink as Hank had instructed, since a new stainless-steel version was soon to be installed. After stretching out the job as long as possible, he returned to find the room straightened and Rachel poised with her purse slung over her shoulder, as if she couldn't wait to escape.

Not the best way to end the evening.

Unless they defused the tension between them, Rachel would insist that Eleanor put her on a different work crew—and that wasn't the outcome he wanted. Getting involved with her might have a boatload of downsides, but there were upsides, too. The spark flaring between them suggested all kinds of interesting possibilities, once they got to know one another better.

But that wasn't going to happen if she bolted.

The question was, what could he do to put her at ease and build some trust? How could he acknowledge the elephant in the room without getting squashed by it?

To buy himself a few moments to cobble together a strategy, he propped his foot on the bottom rung of the ladder and retied the shoe on his prosthetic leg.

His leg.

Could that be his entrée?

His fingers lingered on the shoestring.

Perhaps.

All evening, Rachel had studiously avoided looking at it—even though this guts-exposed model always drew attention. That was the very reason he usually wore it only at home or under slacks. But after Gram had shaken her head at his jeans and warned him about the temperature in the house, he'd made a quick change into shorts without bothering to go through the process of switching legs. Had he known he'd encounter Rachel, however, he'd have taken the time to swap this one out for the more natural-looking version.

But since the leg was the reason they'd gotten off to a rocky start, maybe his choice was providential. It could give him an opening to smooth things out between them and pave the way for next steps. If all went well, it might even open the door to more personal subjects.

Like the attraction crackling between them.

He finished tying the shoe and straightened up without removing his leg from the rung of the ladder. "I would have worn a different model if I'd known you were coming." He kept his tone conversational. "This one tends to freak some people out."

Rachel sent a sideways glance toward his leg. An instant later she yanked it away and peered into her purse, digging for her keys.

In other words, she was doing everything possible not to stare and risk ruffling his feathers again.

In light of their history he couldn't blame her.

But now that he knew her interest wasn't prompted by some kind of morbid curiosity, he didn't care if she looked. In fact, he wanted her to. It was part of who he was. If she couldn't deal with the leg, better to know now.

"Hey."

At his soft word, she stopped pawing through her purse and lifted her chin, her expression wary.

"Are you one of the people who's freaked out by this?" He indicated the metal tube.

Rachel examined his leg, looking more curious

than repulsed. "No. It seems very utilitarian—and sturdy. In fact, it makes me think of that TV program from the '70s about a bionic man."

"That was a bit before your time, wasn't it?"

She shrugged and gave him a sheepish grin. "I like to watch reruns of old TV series. They're better than what's on television now."

"No arguments there. I'm an old-TV-show junkie, too—but I can't run as fast as Steve Austin."

Rachel arched an eyebrow. "I'm impressed. You even remember the character's name."

"Watching old TV shows helped pass the days while I recovered from this." He tapped his leg. "And while I wallowed in self-pity." No need to mention the gnawing guilt that had plagued him in those early days…and still did.

At his candid comment, she scrutinized him. "How did you get past that?"

Some nuance in her quiet, intent tone told him her question wasn't just a polite inquiry. It was almost as if she was seeking an answer for herself.

Did she hold traumatic secrets close to her heart, too?

Fletch rested an elbow on a rung of the ladder as he considered how to answer a question he'd never asked himself. "Honestly? I don't know. For one thing, my medical team didn't put up with a lot of wallowing. They pushed and prodded and got me up and moving. They also sent recovered vets with worse limb losses than mine to visit me. Guys who'd lost both legs above the knees. Or both arms. Or legs and an arm. Talking to them helped me realize I was more fortunate than a lot of people, and that if I worked at it I could have a close-to-normal life. So I did. And I do."

Rachel inspected his leg. "You know, I would never have believed you'd lost a leg if I hadn't seen the prosthesis. But I have a feeling achieving that kind of normalcy involved a whole lot of hard stuff they never showed on *The Six Million Dollar Man*."

"It did." No need to go into detail about the staph infection that had weakened him and slowed his recovery, the hours of prosthetic fittings, the first struggling steps, the rigors—and discouragement—of therapy.

"Since you didn't attend church with Louise last Sunday, I'm thinking prayer wasn't part of your recovery equation."

"Not unless my rantings at the Almighty counted—but those were hardly prayers." Fletch shrugged. "My faith was a battlefield casualty, mortally wounded long before this." He gestured to his leg again.

Based on the subtle disappointment in her eyes, that wasn't the answer she'd hoped to hear. But he wasn't going to lie. How could a loving, merciful God allow the kind of mental and physical horrors he'd witnessed—and endured—during his years as a SEAL?

"I'm sorry you didn't have that to rely on. With all the stuff that's happened in my life, I doubt I would have survived without God in my corner."

All what stuff, beyond her husband's tragic death?

But Rachel moved on, putting the focus back on him. "So may I ask what happened to your leg? Or is that an off-limits topic?"

Fletch's stomach coiled, and he fisted the hand hanging at his side. "I don't talk much about it. Even my family only knows the basics."

"I understand." She edged toward the door and started rooting for her keys again. "I didn't mean to…"

"But I can give you the highlights—or lowlights— if you're interested."

She stopped rummaging in her purse and shot him a surprised look.

The offer took him off guard, too.

Yet if he wanted to build trust, what better way than to share a deeply personal story with her?

"I'm interested."

He gave a curt nod. "Why don't we get out of this hotbox and move to the porch? We might at least pick up a breeze."

Without a word, she preceded him down the hall and waited for him at the front door. He flipped off the lights, pitched their soda cans into the sealed recycle bin in the kitchen and motioned her through the door. After setting the lock as Hank had instructed, he followed her out.

"I guess we'll have to make do with this." He gestured to the steps of the concrete stoop that was framed by a jasmine-covered arbor.

Rachel lowered herself in silence, and he sat next to her.

For a full minute, he let the peace of the night settle over him, hoping it would offset the turbulence in his mind. But try as he might, he couldn't rein in the hard beat of his pulse or the sudden uptick in his respiration.

"I won't be offended if you want to retract your offer."

Rachel's gentle words steadied him.

He could do this.

He *would* do this.

"No. I just needed a minute to pull my thoughts together."

Her arm brushed his. Had she moved closer or simply shifted into a more comfortable position on the hard concrete? No matter. The brief contact further bolstered his resolve.

"It happened in the Middle East, as you already know, on a classified advance-force recon mission. I'd done dozens of those. Never easy, always dangerous, but I was used to the drill. On this night, our mission was to set up a surveillance point above a cluster of huts in the mountains, confirm the presence of one of the local leaders and assess his troop strength so a larger force could go in and round everyone up."

A breeze rustled the leaves of the jasmine above him, infusing the night air with perfume. He drew in a lungful—but the sweet smell wasn't enough to dilute the bitter memories.

Leaning forward, he clasped his hands between his knees and focused on Polaris, bright in the dark sky—a guidepost for centuries to those in need of direction.

If only he had a guidepost like that to help him find his way out of the morass of tangled emotions still lingering from that fateful night.

"It was dark. My partner, Deke, and I were part of a four-man unit. The other pair was a couple hundred yards away. We'd been in position for several hours, and everything was quiet. I was beginning to think our intel was wrong—when out of the blue, chaos erupted." Fletch gripped his knuckles harder and gave voice to the guilt that had haunted him for two and a half years. "And it was all my fault."

The caw of a gull broke the quiet night, and he paused to take a slow, calming breath. He hadn't talked about the incident since the debriefing from his bed in Landstuhl. Not even the shrinks and chaplains who'd visited him at the army hospital in Germany, a world removed from the front lines, had been able to convince him to revisit the horrors once the official interrogation was over.

Yet without even trying, a blonde widow on a barrier island in Georgia had managed better than all the professionals to ease him toward the edge of his emotional cliff.

Go figure.

But the worst was yet to come...and as he hovered on the precipice, his resolve wavered.

Suddenly a gentle hand reached out and came to rest on his knee.

Fletch turned his head. The soft light beside the door behind them left Rachel's face in shadows, but he didn't need illumination to confirm it was filled with compassion and kindness—or to know her perceptive eyes were seeing into his soul despite the darkness.

The temptation to cover her fingers with his was strong. Too strong. If he touched her...who knew what might happen? He needed to get through this first.

Calling on every ounce of his self-control, he refocused on the North Star. "It gets worse. You can bail now if you want to."

"I'm in for the duration."

Swallowing past the lump in his throat, he plunged back into the nightmare. "Earlier in the day, while we were scouting around, two goat herders appeared out of nowhere—an older man and a ten- or eleven-year-old boy. In that area, it was hard to tell the insurgents from the innocent villagers, and there are only two choices in a situation like that: let them go and hope they disappear or take them out on the assumption they'll run straight to the terrorists and report your position."

Her fingers tightened on his knee. "You let them go."

"Yeah. As the squad leader, I made the final call. I had a bad feeling about them, but they weren't armed, and the rules of engagement were clear—don't open fire unless fired upon or until you've positively identified the enemy and have proof of his intentions."

A beat of silence ticked by, and when Rachel spoke, her hushed words were filled with horror. "I can't even imagine being faced with a decision like that. What if you'd decided to…to eliminate the risk, and the old man and child turned out to be innocent?"

"That's why a lot of soldiers end up with PTSD. It's mind-bending to fight a war with a hard-to-identify enemy. Make the wrong choice, buddies die. Make the right choice, people still die." The star shining in the heavens suddenly blurred around the edges. "I made the wrong choice that day, and Deke paid for it—with his life."

Sitting beside the ex-SEAL on the steps of Francis House, Rachel attempted to sort through her jumbled emotions.

Yet hard as she tried, she couldn't come to grips with all he'd told her in time to form a coherent response.

One thing for sure, though.

She didn't have a corner on guilt.

As the silence lengthened, as regret and self-recrimination radiated from the taut man beside her, she struggled to find words that might console. But only trite platitudes came to mind, and as she knew from experience, they were useless.

"Sorry to dump all that on you."

At Fletch's hoarse apology, Rachel shifted toward him. His shadowed face was in profile, his head bowed, his eyes downcast. Misery rolled off him in waves.

"Don't apologize. I feel privileged that you shared your story with me." She hesitated, then leaned down and touched the metal tube of his substitute leg with her free hand, leaving the other one on his knee.

He froze.

"Tell me about this." Somehow she knew the loss of his leg was the lynchpin of the story. This was the reason Deke had died and Fletch bore such guilt.

His gaze remained riveted on her hand.

Five seconds crept by.

Finally, he continued. "It was a grenade. There was a momentary lull in enemy fire, and I heard it hit the ground right in front of the rocks we were behind. I lunged for Deke to shove him down and caught the brunt of the blast—blunt-force trauma to the chest and abdomen and a shredded leg."

He touched the metal rod, his fingers inches from hers. "After I was injured, Deke's best chance was to try to work his way over to the other two members of the squad. I was out of the fight, and the three of them together had better odds of holding their ground until the helo Deke managed to radio for arrived. But SEALs don't leave their buddies behind, and Deke was a SEAL to the core."

His throat worked, and he tipped his head to swipe the sleeve of his T-shirt across his eyes. "The thing is, even with me down, we almost made it. I could hear the bird approaching. Then all at once there was some shouting from the insurgents—and through his night-vision goggles Deke spotted a guy with an RPG."

It took Rachel a moment to pull the acronym out of her memory from all the news stories she'd read. Rocket-propelled grenade. A weapon powerful enough to disable a tank—or take down a helicopter.

"Deke looked at me, said, 'Hang tight, buddy. You're gonna make it,' and disappeared. A minute later I heard an explosion. The helicopter opened fire, and the insurgents scattered. I found out later Deke had low-crawled over the open ground to take out the guy. He succeeded—but one of the insurgents sprayed the area with his machine gun. Deke caught a direct hit."

Pressure built behind Rachel's eyes. Now she understood the depth of Fletch's guilt. The whole disaster had been triggered by his call on the shepherds—a call he'd made despite his gut feeling the two locals were trouble. All because he'd been trying to play by the rules and spare potentially innocent lives.

But an innocent man had died anyway.

"Deke left behind a wife and three-year-old son. I'm David's godfather." Fletch's voice roughened, and he wiped a hand down his face.

The story just kept getting worse.

A tear spilled out of her eye, and she placed her hand over his white knuckles. "I'm so sorry." Her own words came out ragged.

A shudder rippled through him, and he tugged free of her comforting clasp. But before she could retract her hand, he caught it, twined their fingers together...and held on tight.

Only then did he look at her. "Sorry. It's not a pretty story."

The light was too dim to offer a clear view of his features. But the tremor in his words spoke volumes. She'd met the man beside her a mere handful of days ago, but she'd read enough about Navy SEALs to know they didn't shake easily. They learned to control their emotions and possessed both physical and mental strength. She also knew they never showed weakness of any kind, never exposed their vulnerabilities. An Achilles' heel could be used against you.

Yet Fletch had taken the risk of opening up to her tonight, sending a clear message. He trusted her—and cared about her more than such a brief acquaintance should merit.

She felt the same way.

And that was scary.

This trip was supposed to be about relaxation, not romance. She had too many unresolved issues of her own to even think about getting involved with anyone.

Like it or not, though, tonight's story had linked her with Fletch.

"You probably wish you'd left after the soda."

At his comment, she refocused on him. "No." She hesitated, trying to organize her thoughts. "It's just a lot to process. But my instincts tell me you made the best decision you could, based on the information you had. And now that I've heard your story, I'm more impressed than ever by how you've managed to go on with your life. A lot of people would never get past that kind of trauma."

Like her.

After three years, she still hadn't come to grips with her culpability in Mark's death.

Or the death of her child.

Her throat tightened, and she forced herself to swallow her tears. Those were not subjects she wanted to think about right now. Tonight, the focus needed to stay on Fletch.

"I moved on with the externals. Not so much with the internals." He stroked his thumb over the back of her hand, watching her with a disconcerting intensity. He might not be wearing night-vision goggles, but she had a feeling he was seeing her face a lot more clearly than she was seeing his. "I'm thinking that may be starting to change, though."

Because of you.

The unspoken words vibrated between them, as potent—and unsettling—as if he'd given voice to them.

A wave of panic rippled through her. "Look, Fletch, I'm not…"

"Hey." He held up a hand. "I stopped speaking where I did for a reason. We only met a couple of weeks ago. I don't even know your favorite color or your birthday or what flavor of ice cream you prefer or whether you like sports. None of that important stuff."

One side of his mouth twitched, and the touch of humor helped smooth out the tension in her shoulders as he continued. "But I do know I'm glad our paths crossed, even if our first meeting was memorable for all the wrong reasons. So why don't we take this a day at a time? We can paint together here. Maybe try the beach thing again. Bring Bandit if you like. We'll keep it low-key and casual. If we decide to part ways at the end of our stays on Jekyll, so be it. If we don't…we'll cross that bridge when we come to it. What do you say?"

Rachel tried to examine his proposal logically, but the lean, firm fingers interlaced with hers had somehow disengaged the left side of her brain. Might as well go with the flow.

"Yes."

"That wasn't a hard sell." There was the tiniest hint of laughter in his inflection, a welcome reprieve from the somberness of moments before.

"What you're suggesting makes sense. Besides, I have some issues of my own to work through."

"Maybe we can talk about them sometime."

"Maybe." Fletch might be brave enough to share his feelings of guilt, but she'd have to dig deep to find that kind of courage.

"Ready to call it a night?" He stood, his hand still linked with hers.

"Yes."

He pulled her to her feet.

She waited for him to release her.

He didn't.

As they stood under the jasmine-draped arbor, the sweet scent filling the night air, Rachel tipped her head back and looked into his dark brown eyes. Now that they were standing sideways to the porch light, she could make out his features. Though their conversation had lightened during the last exchange, traces of pain and remorse and blame were etched into his forehead and at the corners of his mouth. None of those lines had been there earlier in the evening.

"Could you use a quick hug?" Her offer came unbidden, surprising her.

Without hesitating, he reached out and pulled her close.

Rachel stepped into his embrace, against a rock-solid chest where a heart thumped hard and a bit too fast against her ear, into arms that were strong yet gentle as they held her.

Far too soon, he eased back. Then he lifted one hand, plucked a spray of jasmine and handed it to her. "Let's end the night on a sweet note."

She lifted the blossoms to her nose and inhaled, knowing the scent of jasmine would be linked to this night for the rest of her life.

Only after he walked her back to her car did he release her hand. "Be careful."

"I will."

She fumbled the key, but after two tries she managed to insert it in the lock and start the engine. Once she backed onto the street and accelerated toward Aunt El's, she glanced in the rearview mirror.

Fletch was still standing in the driveway, looking after her.

A few seconds later, she turned onto the road to Aunt El's and he disappeared from view.

But his final words lingered in the jasmine-infused air.

Be careful.

Good advice—and it applied to far more than her short drive home.

Chapter Eight

His let's-keep-things-low-key-and-casual-but-move-forward plan wasn't working.

Fletch wiped a smear of pale green paint off his hand and looked across the living room. Rachel was back on trim detail—but so was Marilyn Cooper. In the adjacent dining room, Delores and Al were tackling the walls. Hank had spent most of the evening hanging a swing on the front porch.

According to the countdown board posted in the kitchen, the Mitchell family was arriving in eighteen days—and the place was crawling with volunteers for the third session in a row. With much work still to do, the ranks swelled day by day.

That was good for the project.

Not so good for him.

He hadn't had two minutes alone with Rachel since the night he'd spilled his guts.

Instead of quiet evenings under the jasmine vine

out front, sharing a Coke and getting to know each other better, they'd been eating the ice cream Hank hauled in every night for the crew.

At least he'd learned her favorite flavor: mint chocolate chip.

Despite the frozen treats and the now-functioning air conditioner, however, he was getting hot under the collar. Gram's wrist was progressing well. Soon she wouldn't need him anymore—if she'd ever needed him at all—and his clients were clamoring for more face time. In less than a month, he'd be on his way back to Norfolk.

Where were Gram and Eleanor's matchmaking schemes when he needed them?

Apparently the next move was up to him.

Tossing the rag aside, he crossed to Rachel. She was intent on the woodwork, lower lip caught between her teeth, faint creases scoring her brow.

"You have the concentration of a SEAL."

Her hand jerked, leaving a white slash on the new green paint. She grabbed the damp rag that was draped over the tray of the ladder and scrubbed it away before she gave him a disgruntled look. "And you have the stealth."

"Our stock in trade." He smiled.

She smiled back.

The lady had a killer smile—and he wanted to see a whole lot more of it.

Fletch checked over his shoulder. Marilyn was on

the far side of the room, painting the molding around the door of the coat closet, ear buds firmly in place as she listened to the golden oldies she favored. Perfect. The congregation at Gram's church seemed close-knit, and he didn't want any spies reporting to her.

He turned back to Rachel. "I was hoping our painting sessions would give us a chance to get to know each other better, but it's beginning to feel like Grand Central Station in here."

"I noticed."

"So why don't we spend a couple of hours on the beach tomorrow? I'll supply the snacks and drinks. You can bring Bandit and the infamous Frisbee."

She grinned. "If food is involved, a Bandit-less outing would be better. His mooching can get annoying."

"Sold."

"And let's make it South Dunes. I'm manning Aunt El's gallery tomorrow morning, so why don't I meet you there at one?"

"That should work—but why don't you give me your cell number in case anything comes up?" He jotted the numbers as she recited them, then pocketed the slip of paper. "I'm fine with South Dunes, but wouldn't it be more convenient for you if we went to the beach by your place?"

"Yes—but far less comfortable. Aunt El's supposed to be on duty at the gallery all afternoon, but I wouldn't put it past her to stick the 'gone shelling' sign in the door and sneak home for an hour to spy on us from her sky room."

That was a new one.

"What's a 'sky room'?"

"Her living room has a vaulted ceiling, and there's a balcony near the top with two chairs and a big window that overlooks the ocean. The arthritis in her knees keeps her at sea level most of the time, but she might make the climb if she gets suspicious—a strong possibility, since I haven't been to the beach a whole lot except for the first few days."

Fletch studied the faint shadows under her eyes. "This hasn't been much of a vacation for you, has it? Teaching classes at the hotel, helping out at Eleanor's gallery, pitching in here, visiting the hospital."

"At least the hospital part is over."

"What's the latest with Madeleine?"

"I got a note from her mother yesterday." She tucked some renegade wisps of hair back into her braid. "It sounds like she and her husband had some long talks while they kept vigil at the hospital. She's going to request a position at work that requires less travel and has more reasonable hours, and they're going to give their marriage another try."

"So your prayers were answered."

"Yes—though not in the way I expected. Appendicitis wasn't on my wish list." She shrugged. "But that's how God works sometimes."

The front door banged open, and Hank entered

with a large white bag and a grin. "The Good Humor man is here."

As the other volunteers converged on him, Fletch steadied the ladder so Rachel could descend. "Your mint chocolate chip awaits."

"What did you get tonight?"

"Rocky road."

She stepped onto the floor and looked up at him. For a moment he thought she was going to comment on his flavor choice. Instead, she wiped her hands on a rag and headed for Hank. "Better get it before it melts."

Propping his fists on his hips, Fletch watched her walk away. She was still being careful around him. Still feeling her way and trying not to offend.

They needed to get past that—even if he had to deep-six his low-key-and-casual plan and ratchet things up, take a more aggressive approach.

Because before he left Jekyll Island, he intended to log some serious miles in this relationship.

"The house is coming along wonderfully, isn't it?" Eleanor poured a glass of orange juice as she monitored the waffle iron, a hopeful Bandit planted by her side.

"Yes, it is." Rachel closed the refrigerator door and set the butter and syrup on the table. "I don't think you have to worry anymore about disappointing the rest of the families scheduled to visit."

"A lot of the credit for that goes to you and Fletch."

"Not true. More volunteers show up every day. There were six of us last night."

"I have to tip my hat to Reverend Carlson for that. He's been making a plea from the pulpit every Sunday and at every event during the week, lathering on the guilt in that subtle way of his. But Hank tells me you two young people are running circles around everyone else."

"He's exaggerating." Rachel peeked at her watch as she dug through the utensil drawer for knives and forks. Five hours until she met Fletch at the beach.

A lifetime.

Lucky thing she was working at the Painted Pelican until noon. Dealing with the customers in Aunt El's gallery should help pass the morning.

"No, hyperbole isn't Hank's style. He's a call-'em-as-I-see-'em kind of guy. He says you and Fletch make a great team, by the way."

Rachel let that pass.

"But I must say, you're looking a bit tired. I hope you're planning to take it easy this afternoon."

Rachel passed out the silverware, keeping her tone casual. "I'm weighing a few options. I haven't made much progress on the suspense novel I brought with me, and I want to stop in and see the new exhibit at the Sea Turtle Center Louise told me about after services last Sunday. What are you going to do with your free morning?"

Sending her a shrewd look, Eleanor snagged the waffle with a fork, plopped it on a plate and set it on the table, Bandit on her heels. "I'm weighing a few options, too."

What was that supposed to mean?

As Rachel slid into her seat and cut off a pat of butter, she sent the older woman a surreptitious glance. Had someone at Francis House overheard her and Fletch setting up their rendezvous and reported back to Eleanor?

Or had she given it away herself just now with her evasive answer?

She spread the butter over the waffle, watching it melt and infiltrate the grooves as Bandit licked his lips. Either explanation was possible. Everyone in the small congregation knew everyone else, and the grapevine was no doubt as active as the Energizer Bunny. Plus, Aunt El had an uncanny ability to ferret out subliminal messages.

On the other hand, maybe she was being paranoid.

"There's some of that tasty almond chicken salad left, if you want to have it for lunch when you get back." Eleanor rooted through the fridge. "Potato salad, too."

She didn't need lunch, not if Fletch was bringing snacks.

"I might grab a bite somewhere while I'm out."

Eleanor closed the refrigerator, retrieved her own waffle and sat beside her, breaking off a piece for

Bandit. The retriever scarfed it down, and she patted his head. "Eating alone isn't much fun. There's plenty in the fridge for two, if you want to ask someone to join you."

"Someone" being Fletch. She didn't know anyone else on the island well enough to invite to lunch.

So her aunt might not suspect anything about the beach outing after all.

"I don't mind eating alone." Rachel opened the bottle of syrup and squeezed it over her waffle.

"Louise told me Fletch is partial to potato salad—and blondes."

Her fingers tightened on the bottle, and syrup spewed out.

"Oh, my word." Eleanor stared at the glob of sticky maple sweetness oozing in all directions from the center of the waffle. "Isn't that a little much?"

Yeah, it was.

Both the syrup and the commentary.

Eleanor might not know for certain that she had a rendezvous planned, and she and Louise hadn't tried to set them up since that first night at Francis House, but it was clear they hadn't lost interest in promoting a match between their respective younger relatives.

Rachel set the bottle on the table and tried to barricade the widening pool of syrup with her knife.

Curious thing about their well-meaning interference, though. She no longer minded it as much as she once had—because she liked Fletch. Enough that, if the right opening came up, she might consider sharing with him the parts of her past she never talked about.

Maybe even today.

Tipping the waffle on its side, Rachel scraped away the excess syrup as best she could, cut off a bite and gave it a tentative chew.

Yuck. Too sweet.

But it wasn't sweet enough to offset the sudden acrid taste of fear.

If the opportunity did arise, could she be as open and candid with him as he'd been with her?

More important—*should* she be as open and candid? Was it smart to step into the future while she still had one foot in the past?

The answer eluded her.

She could only pray that when the time came, God would give her the guidance she needed to make a wise choice.

Talk about slim pickings.

No wonder Gram did the bulk of her shopping in Brunswick.

Fists planted on hips, Fletch surveyed the aisles of the island's single, small grocery store. There wasn't much chance he'd find a selection of gourmet cheeses in this bare-bones places. As for a fancy paté to impress Rachel—forget it. He'd be lucky if they stocked more than saltines, American cheese and summer sausage. A few strawberries would be a nice touch… but he wasn't holding his breath for those, either.

His phone began to vibrate against his hip as he approached the dairy section, and he pulled it off while scanning the meager cheese display. A fast trip to Brunswick might be in his immediate future. Too bad he'd waited until eleven o'clock to round up provisions for their beach date.

The phone vibrated again, and Fletch cast a distracted glance at caller ID.

Deke's wife?

He frowned.

These days, he was always the one who called her.

Was there an emergency of some sort?

Pulse skittering, he punched the talk button. "Lisa? What's wrong?"

"Nothing. We're fine, Fletch. Sorry. I didn't mean to alarm you. Has it been that long since I called?"

His heart settled down, and he exhaled as the refrigerated air from the dairy case cooled his back. "A while—but I know you're busy. How's the day care business?"

"It's working out great. I get to keep David with me all day and make a reasonable living at the same time. I couldn't ask for a more ideal situation."

Yeah, she could.

If all had gone as she and Deke planned, she'd be a stay-at-home mom who didn't have to worry about making ends meet or do all the heavy lifting to provide for her son's future.

Lisa spoke as if she'd read his mind. "Hey…David and I are doing okay. Don't worry about us so much." A woman reached past him and grabbed a container of eggs, lifting the lid to inspect the contents. One was broken. "How's your grandmother?"

"Her wrist is healing well."

The woman put the eggs back and repeated the drill until she found a perfect dozen.

"I'm glad to hear that. Listen…I was wondering if you might have some time for a short visit. I'd really like to see you."

He wandered away from the dairy section, stopping beside a small display of fresh fruit. "Sure. I was planning to drive up to Savannah before I went home. How are your parents?"

"Better since I gave in to their not-so-subtle nudges to move closer. I have to admit it's nice for David to have grandparents nearby."

Especially since he didn't have a father.

"Yeah." Fletch clenched his teeth.

"The thing about getting together—I was wondering if you had some time today."

"Today?" As best he could recall, Savannah was close to a hundred miles north. No way could he fit both that trip and a date with Rachel into his afternoon schedule. But Lisa wouldn't ask if it wasn't important. "I could get up there later this evening. Would that work?"

"I can save you the gas—and the trouble. I'm about an hour away from the island, heading your direction. I was going to surprise you and drop in unannounced, but then I figured I better make sure you were available."

Fletch picked up a lemon from the display beside him and weighed it in his hand, trying to make sense of her impromptu trip. "You're driving down just to talk to me?"

"I'll explain when I get there. I know it's short notice, and I don't mean to inconvenience you, but I'd really appreciate it if you could spare an hour."

"Of course I can." His date with Rachel would have to wait. He'd promised himself he'd be there whenever Lisa needed him, and he wasn't going to renege on that commitment. "There's a restaurant on the main circle road called Fins. You can't miss it. Cut straight across the island after you come off the bridge, and hang a left on Beachview Drive. I'll meet you there at twelve-fifteen."

"You don't have to feed me."

"I need to eat, too."

"In that case…thanks. I'll see you soon."

Slowly Fletch slid the phone back on his belt. Lisa hadn't sounded upset, but something was up. There'd been an unsettling undercurrent of emotion in her voice. Nervousness, perhaps? Uncertainty? Anxiety?

Was she bringing him bad news?

"Hey, mister...you gonna make some lemonade?"

Pulling himself back to the present, Fletch looked down at the little blond-haired boy standing in front of him. The youngster was about the same age as David.

"What?"

The boy pointed to the lemon in his hand.

Fletch set it back on the display and took a step away. The last thing he needed in his life was another lemon.

"No. I was just holding it."

"My mom makes good lemonade. You have to add a lot of sugar, though, or your mouth puckers up like this." The boy contorted his face.

A young woman hurried over, a toddler in tow, and took the little boy's hand. "Come on, honey. Don't bother the man." She sent him an apologetic look. "Sorry about that."

"No problem."

"You should make some lemonade." The boy called the advice over his shoulder as his mother tugged him away. "Lemons are a lot easier to eat if you sweeten them up."

Out of the mouths of babes...

If only it was that easy.

Scratching shopping off his agenda, Fletch exited the store—hoping Lisa wasn't about to add one more lemon to his collection.

* * *

"I'm sure you'll enjoy this immensely, Mrs. Gardner." Rachel stole a peek at her watch. Just an hour and a half to go before her beach date with Fletch… but the way this woman had been languishing over her purchase, she'd be hemming and hawing for another thirty minutes. At least Aunt El could relieve her of duty—and dithering customers—once she arrived.

The sooner the better.

Cocking her head, the woman examined the impressionist seascape for the dozenth time. "But are you certain it will blend with the colors in my living room? Let me show you the photos again."

Rachel controlled the impulse to roll her eyes. Should she give the woman a quick art-appreciation lesson? Tell her paintings weren't like a lamp or a throw cushion, that one bought art for its inherent beauty, not as a décor item? That you were supposed to draw attention to it, make it the centerpiece of a room, not hope it blended in?

She eyed the woman's outfit—pink flats edged with teal trim. Pink, white and teal tropical-print skirt. White top with teal buttons and teal trim around the collar. Even her necklace carried out the color scheme.

Give it up, Rachel. Just listen and nod and hope she buys the painting.

Half an hour later, as the woman finally pried her

fingers off her credit card, the bell jingled over the front door and Aunt El bustled in.

Hallelujah!

Rachel rang up the purchase, assured the woman the painting would be packed and shipped the next day and sent her on her way. Before the door clicked shut behind her, she was reaching for her purse.

"Tough customer...or places to go?" Eleanor tucked her own purse under the front counter.

"Let me put it this way. If the pros and cons of Paul Revere's ride had been debated for as long as Mrs. Gardner waffled about that one painting, the opening shots of the Revolutionary War wouldn't have been fired in Concord."

Eleanor chuckled. "I get more than my share of that type. All I can say is, you deserve a relaxing afternoon, whatever you decide to do. A trip to the beach might help."

Don't look at her, Rachel. Your face will give you away.

"I'll have to think about that." She kept her head bent as she dug for her keys and started for the door. "See you tonight."

Once outside, she headed for her car, pulling out her phone. If she'd been smart, she'd have left the ringer on audible while she was tending the shop. An incoming call would have given her an excuse to break away from Mrs. Gardner for a moment.

Not that she'd had much chance of being saved by

the bell, however. Few people from Richmond called during her visits to Jekyll Island, and she didn't have any friends here except for Fletch.

Her afternoon date.

A trill of anticipation pranced through her as she turned on her phone, skimmed the screen and began to slide it back into her purse.

Wait.

Had the screen indicated a missed call?

She retracted her hand and looked again. Yes. From an unfamiliar number.

After pressing the auto-lock for her car, Rachel tapped in her voice-mail access code and picked up her pace. By the time she changed clothes and touched up her hair and makeup, the next hour was going to whiz by—and she didn't intend to keep Fletch waiting.

"You have one new message. Wednesday, June 27, 11:30 a.m."

As she pulled open her car door, a familiar voice began speaking. "Rachel, it's Fletch. I'm sorry to have to do this, but I need to bail on our beach date. Something…personal…has come up. I'll give you a call later this afternoon and explain."

She froze, hand on the door.

Fletch was canceling their date?

For *personal* reasons?

Like what?

It couldn't have anything to do with Louise. If the

older woman had had some sort of setback, he'd have told her. There would be no reason to keep that a secret, not when she and Aunt El were so close.

Was it possible he'd simply gotten cold feet, decided he didn't want things between them to get any cozier? Maybe he was having second thoughts—or regrets—about all he'd shared with her.

Despite the cloudless blue sky and brilliant sun, the day suddenly seemed a little less bright.

The staccato beep of a horn prodded her forward, toward her Focus. But once she reached it, Rachel paused again. Taking a deep breath, she squared her shoulders.

She would not allow a broken date with a man she'd met a mere three weeks ago ruin a beautiful June day on Jekyll Island.

Jaw set, she slid into her car, started the engine and backed out of her parking spot. Why not treat herself to lunch at her favorite restaurant? Better to dine alone than sulk around the house all afternoon thinking about the date that might have been. If he wanted to give her an explanation and reschedule, fine. If not…she'd survive. Why complicate her life by getting involved with a man who lived in a different city, anyway?

Because he's nice…and he's hot…and you're attracted to him?

Rachel pulled onto the main road and cranked up the air, aiming all the ducts at her flushed cheeks.

Fine. She could admit all that. What woman wouldn't be attracted to a guy with dark good looks and a flattering willingness to trust her with his secrets?

But he was also pushing her out of her comfort zone.

Maybe this canceled date was a reminder that she needed to think about how involved she wanted to get with Louise's grandson before she went down a path she might regret. Maybe she should be grateful for this opportunity to consider next steps—assuming he wanted to take any.

Shoving that thought aside, Rachel swung into the crowded lot at Fins. For once, fate was kind to her. A car pulled out of a spot near the entrance, and she claimed it with a quick twist of the wheel.

After setting her locks, she walked up the curving sidewalk toward the seaside entrance of the restaurant, scanning the terrace as she approached. Might her spurt of good fortune include finding an empty table under one of the umbrellas?

Nope. The place was packed.

Just as she started to turn toward the door that led to inside seating, a couple at a table in the far corner of the terrace caught her eye. The thirtysomething brunette facing her wasn't familiar, and the man was partly hidden by a waiter talking to the people at an adjacent table, but those broad shoulders and that deep brown hair…

The waiter shifted, and Rachel's heart faltered. Was that…?

The man angled slightly to speak to the waiter, giving her a partial view of his profile.

It was Fletch.

The bottom dropped out of her stomach.

He'd canceled their date to meet another woman for lunch at *their* place.

Backing away, Rachel tucked herself behind one of the potted palms that rimmed the path, claiming a spot beside the ever-lurking seagulls as she tried to process this new development.

Don't jump to conclusions or assume the worst, Rachel. There might be a reasonable explanation. Keep an open mind. Listen to what he has to say when he calls later. Give him the benefit of the doubt. Be mature. You're a grown…

A seagull flapped at her feet, and she looked down.

The bird had apparently mistaken her for a statue and deposited a gift on the toe of her leather flat.

As she shooed him away and dug through her purse for some tissues, Rachel grimaced at the pile of poop.

What a fitting end to her morning.

She just hoped it wasn't an omen for the rest of her day.

Chapter Nine

Fletch handed his menu back to the waiter and inspected Lisa as she took a sip of water. What was it about her that had changed in the eight months since their last in-person conversation? Yes, her hair was a bit shorter, she'd gained back a few of the pounds she'd lost after Deke died, and she was wearing more makeup than usual—but none of those alterations accounted for the subtle difference in her.

The change was deeper than cosmetic.

"I feel like a frog under a microscope." She flashed him a tentative smile. "You've had me pinned with that piercing, analytical SEAL look ever since I arrived. It's very intimidating."

He forced up the corners of his mouth. "I'm not trying to intimidate you. But I am curious."

"I figured you would be." Lisa straightened her cutlery. Flicked a crumb off the table top. Smoothed a finger along the crease in her napkin.

Her stall tactics weren't helping his blood pressure.

After another few seconds of silence, he took charge. Might as well get this over with. "So what's up?"

Her lips quirked. "I see you're still a typical let's-cut-to-the-chase-and-dispense-with-the-small-talk SEAL."

"Guilty as charged."

Lisa took a deep breath, folded her hands and swallowed. "I wish there was some easy way to lead up to this, but if there is, I haven't figured it out—and I've been trying for three days. So I'll just put it on the table, and then we can discuss it."

Fletch braced himself. Whatever was coming was going to upend his world.

Again.

"I'm getting married."

As the three simple words hovered in the air, all other sounds receded. The clatter of silverware, the laughter of their fellow diners, the muted crash of the surf in the distance, the ring of a cell phone...they registered only at some peripheral level of awareness as he grappled with her bombshell.

The woman who'd loved Deke with a fierce, singular passion, who'd borne his beloved son, who'd mourned his loss with an almost palpable grief, was going to give her heart—and her loyalties—to another man.

It wasn't computing.

"You're shocked, aren't you?"

Fletch heard her question.

But he had no clue how to respond.

"Of course you are." Lisa leaned closer, her expression intent—and troubled. "You want the truth? I'm shocked, too. I wasn't looking for a new man in my life. I love Deke—and I always will. His place in my heart belongs to him and him alone forever. It hasn't been easy these past two and a half years, but David and I were making it on our own and life was beginning to settle into a new normal. Then I met Mitch…and everything changed."

The waiter appeared, and she paused while he set their plates in front of them.

That brief break gave Fletch a chance to absorb her news.

Yet he still couldn't come up with a response.

As the waiter departed, Lisa reached over and touched his hand. "I don't know how to explain this, Fletch, except that when I met Mitch, the darkness began to lift. It was like I'd been living in a cave, and suddenly I began to see glimmers of light in the distance." She searched his face. "Have you ever had anyone walk into your life, and somehow you knew things were going to be different? Better?"

An image of Rachel flashed through his mind.

Yeah, he had.

But he'd never pledged his love to someone else.

Shouldn't it be different once you did that? Shouldn't that kind of bond linger even past death?

"I know what you're thinking." Lisa withdrew her hand and stared down at her shrimp Caesar salad. "You're thinking I'm betraying Deke by falling in love with someone else. I thought that at first, too." She lifted her chin and locked gazes with him. "But I don't anymore. After I met Mitch, I began to realize that since Deke died, I've been going through the motions of life. I've been marking the days, nothing more. And that wasn't fair to David…or to me. I've also come to believe it's not fair to the memory of Deke, either. Do you?"

Talk about being put on the spot.

Fletch took a sip of water. Cleared his throat. Picked up his fork. Put it down again.

Lisa waited him out.

He groped for words that would placate without condoning. "You have to do what you think is right, Lisa." Lame…but the best he could come up with.

"You think I'm wrong."

"I'm not judging you."

"Yes, you are. I knew you would. That's why I wanted to tell you the news in person. Because after a lot of prayer and soul searching, I've concluded that neither of us should feel guilty about moving on. If Deke could weigh in on this issue, do you think he'd want me to live the rest of my life alone? Do you think he'd want his son to grow up without a father? Do you think he'd want you to spend your life mourning him—and feeling guilty over a decision that could have gone either way?"

A muscle in his jaw ticced, and he fisted a hand in his lap, keeping his features neutral. No one knew about the shepherds except the men on the mission... and Rachel. He'd never shared the particulars with Lisa.

Fletch sent her a cautious look. "What decision?"

Her eyes never wavered. "I found out about the shepherds a few months ago. One of the guys who was in your recon squad that night stopped by while he was in the area to offer his condolences and see how I was doing."

Lisa knew he'd caused Deke's death—yet she was sitting here talking to him?

His throat tightened, and the edges of his vision blurred. "I'm sorry. I should have told you myself."

"I'm glad you didn't. If I'd heard the story two and a half years ago, I might have blamed you."

"You would have had every right to do that."

"No, I wouldn't." Lisa gripped his hand. "Listen to me, Fletch. I was the wife of a SEAL. I know what you guys faced on the battlefield. I know the kind of gut-wrenching, split-second decisions you had to make, often without full information. What happened that night wasn't your fault. Deke would say the same thing. So would you, if your positions were reversed. You did the best you could under the circumstances."

Those were almost the same words Rachel had used.

"And here's the thing. Neither of us can bring Deke back. Yesterday's over. Done. Nothing we can do will change that. But we *can* make choices about tomorrow. I choose love over loneliness—and in my heart, I believe Deke would approve of that. When you love someone, you want them to be happy. And Deke loved me with all his heart...as I loved him."

Fletch studied her. Was she sincere, or was she trying to rationalize her decision? Apparently the former, based on her demeanor. She seemed at peace with her choice. Confident about it, even.

"I can't argue with your conviction, Lisa."

"Because it's genuine—and right. You were his best friend. You know how much he loved life. How he lived in the moment. How he embraced everything good that came his way and brushed aside the bad. He chose joy. I intend to pass that legacy on to David, and to honor it in my own life. I think you should do the same. Choose joy, Fletch. Let the guilt go. Give it to God and move on."

Give it to God.

Was that what it would take to unburden himself from the yoke of guilt? Was God the spiritual and emotional North Star he'd been seeking all these months?

Maybe. Both Gram and Rachel had suggested as much.

But how did you repair a relationship that was in tatters?

"You folks need anything else?"

At the waiter's question, Fletch looked up. A serving of absolution would be nice. Too bad it wasn't on the menu. "We're fine. Thanks." As the man walked away, Fletch refocused on Lisa. "You've given me a lot to think about."

"I hope you do more than think. You should make your peace with the past and find a good woman to love."

"You sound like my grandmother."

"Then she's a smart woman. Speaking from a sisterly point of view, you're great husband material. Plus, you'd be a wonderful father. David adores you."

Fletch ignored the sudden, painful pang in his heart. "I appreciate the vote of confidence. And on the subject of father material…I want to hear more about this man you're planning to marry."

Eyes twinkling, Lisa picked up her fork and plunged into her salad. "Prepare to have your ear bent."

While he worked his way through his grilled mahimahi, she made good on her warning—and an hour and a half later, as she finished off a slice of cheesecake, she was still going strong.

Fletch found himself smiling at her animation.

This Mitch sounded like a decent guy, and if he brought joy back into her life, who was he to find fault?

Joy.

That was why she looked different.

Lisa was glowing—just as she used to when Deke was alive.

And all at once Fletch knew she was right. This is what Deke would have wanted for the woman he loved. The time for weeping was past.

Perhaps for both of them.

When he finally said goodbye to her in the parking lot with a kiss on the cheek, a promise to attend the wedding and his sincere best wishes, she gripped his hands and held on tight.

"Thank you for taking the news so well."

"Thank you for not hating me."

"I gave my negative feelings to God long ago."

More God talk.

Fletch tugged his hands away and shoved them in his pockets. "You make starting over sound easy."

A shadow crossed her face, dimming her glow. "It's not. It takes a lot of hard work and an openness to the opportunities He sends your way. Six years ago, I would never have foreseen the future that's now stretching before me. But God's plans don't always mesh with ours."

Had she and Rachel compared notes or what?

Lisa touched his arm. "Give Him another chance, Fletch. You won't be sorry."

"I'll consider it." It was the best he could offer.

"Don't labor over it. Just do it. Life is too short to waste time on regrets and what-ifs." She slid into the driver's seat, and when she lifted her face to him, the glow was back. "I'll call you soon with more details about the wedding."

"I'll be there, whenever it is. Give David a hug for me." With that, he closed her door, stepped back and watched her drive away—envying the joy Mitch had resurrected in her life.

Might Rachel have the power do the same for him?

Maybe—except for the stumbling block he'd shared with no one. Would his secret turn her off… or would she be able to accept it as she'd accepted the loss of his leg?

Hard to say. And it was too soon to find out. Things would have to get a lot more serious between them before he shared that confidence.

In any case, after his emotional lunch with Lisa, today wasn't the day to dwell on that question.

For now, he needed a long walk on the beach to think about a whole lot of other things…including his relationship with God.

With a sigh, Rachel adjusted her sunglasses and surveyed the narrowing expanse of deserted beach from the access bridge over the dunes near Aunt El's.

"I guess we waited too long to take our walk." She leaned down and gave Bandit a distracted pat.

He responded with a pitiful whimper.

"Yeah, I hear you. I'm disappointed, too. But the tide's coming in too fast. The steps will be under water in twenty minutes."

Too bad she hadn't checked the tide table when she'd arrived home from Fins instead of plunging into an impromptu bathroom-cleaning frenzy at Francis House.

At the time, though, attacking grungy grout had seemed a perfect follow-up to a canceled date, another woman and seagull poop.

Unfortunately, physical labor hadn't helped her sort through her jumbled emotions. All she had to show for her efforts were a few chipped nails and a cut across her knuckles from a broken tile.

The suspense novel in her room was sounding better and better.

As she did a one-eighty to retrace her steps across the bridge, a sudden movement registered in her peripheral vision. Shading her eyes, she peered into the distance. A guy was sitting on the beach, dressed in clothes much too posh for getting up close and personal with sand and surf. Tan slacks, dress shoes, a blue oxford shirt rolled up to the elbows…

Blue oxford shirt?

Like the kind Fletch had been wearing at Fins?

Rachel squinted, trying to make out his profile.

A moment later, he turned slightly her direction to pick up something beside him, then hurled it into the encroaching sea.

It was Fletch all right.

She planted her hands on her hips and stared. What was he doing on the beach in dress-up clothes? How come his Explorer wasn't parked near the access bridge? Where was his lunch companion? Why hadn't he called her, as he'd promised? His lunch had to have ended two or three hours ago.

And why had he picked *her* beach to sit on, when there were so many other choices?

Stymied, Rachel retreated a few paces, keeping him in sight. She ought to go back to Aunt El's. If he wanted company, he'd have called or stopped by.

Go home, Rachel. Let the man alone.

Sound advice—and she'd follow it. Even if her heart was urging her to do something stupid, like stroll along and pretend she'd stumbled across him.

How juvenile was that?

Turning her back on the sea, she marched herself home, Bandit moping along behind her.

Yet once she was inside the door, her gaze strayed toward the stairs leading to the sky room. From up there, with Aunt El's binoculars, she could get a closer look at him. But wasn't that kind of like… spying?

No. According to that suspense book she was

reading, anything people did in public was fair game for observation.

Quashing the debate between her conscience and her curiosity, Rachel took the stairs at a jog with Bandit on her heels. At the top, she grabbed Aunt El's binoculars and pointed them at Fletch.

He was sitting in the exact same position, knees pulled up, still tossing stuff—pieces of driftwood, shells, what?—into the sea. But with the binoculars, she could pick up a few other pertinent details invisible to the unaided eye.

Like the weary slump of his shoulders—and the force of his pitching. It was almost as if he was angry.

Or hurting.

Rachel lowered the binoculars and caught her bottom lip between her teeth.

"So Bandit…do you think it's possible he chose that spot on purpose, hoping I'd see him and wander out? Or is that a stretch?"

The golden retriever gave a quick bark that sounded like a laugh.

She wrinkled her nose at him. "Thanks for the reality check." Of course it was a stretch. How many times had she herself gotten disoriented while walking on the beach during her first visit? With most of the landmarks hidden by the dunes, one section of golden sand looked much like another.

Once more she lifted the binoculars. Fletch seemed so alone…and lonely. His lunch with the brunette had appeared to be quite cozy, but as near as she could recall, neither had seemed that happy. Their expressions had been serious. Nor was the woman anywhere to be seen now. Had she delivered some sort of bad news?

Rachel set the binoculars back on the small table by the window and debated her options as she descended to the main level. She could forget Fletch was on the beach and read her mystery novel...or solve the mystery of their broken date by joining him. She could simply say she'd seen him from the bridge—no need to mention the sky room—and gauge his receptiveness to her company. Worst case, he'd tell her to get lost.

Could that be any worse than her past few hours scrubbing grout and wondering what was going on?

No way.

Without giving herself a chance to reconsider, Rachel exited the house, leaving a disappointed Bandit whining on the other side of the door. For the second time in ten minutes she crossed the bridge, continuing down the stairs and across the sand toward the solitary figure.

Hoping she wasn't about to make a second major faux pas on Aunt El's beach.

Chapter Ten

The closer Rachel got to Fletch, the slower she walked.

This was a bad idea.

A really bad idea.

If he'd wanted to talk to her, he'd have called.

Instead, he'd come to the beach alone. Meaning he didn't want company.

And why was she so anxious to intrude, anyway? Hadn't she told Gram in no uncertain terms that she hadn't come to Jekyll looking for romance?

So why was she seeking out the very man who was undermining that conviction?

Rachel stopped, her toes sinking into the sand, her confidence eroding as fast as the beach. Better to beat a hasty retreat before he spotted her. As long as his focus remained fixed on the distant horizon, she should be able to…

Fletch's head swiveled toward her, almost as if he'd sensed her presence.

Drat.

She was stuck.

Lifting a hand in greeting, she started forward again, aiming a weak smile his direction.

He didn't respond.

Her mouth quivered, but she kept walking.

She stopped a few feet away, careful not to further invade his space. "I saw you from the bridge." She gestured behind her. "I was going to take a walk, but the tide was against me. In case you didn't notice, you're about to get stranded."

The crevices on his forehead deepened as he did a quick sweep of the area around him, where the encroaching water was pinning him into a small crescent of beach backed by a breakwater of huge boulders.

"Thanks for the warning." He resettled his sunglasses, as if to ensure his eyes were hidden from her view. "I should be able to squeeze out a few more minutes, though."

No invitation to join him.

No explanation about their broken date.

No conversation, period.

This had definitely been a bad idea.

"Well…don't wait too long or you won't be able to reach the steps." Rachel began to edge back. "Are you parked far away?"

"I'm not sure. I took a walk after lunch and lost track of the time."

She stopped. "You walked all the way here from Fins?"

His eyebrows rose, and for the first time she sensed she had his full attention. "How do you know I ate at Fins?"

The sudden heat in her cheeks had nothing to do with the late-afternoon sun sinking in the west.

"Um…" There was no way out except honesty. "After I got your message, I decided to treat myself to lunch. I saw you and…your friend…on the terrace."

"I didn't see you."

Because you were so intent on her.

"I, uh, didn't stay. It was too crowded."

Fletch studied her, then exhaled. "Why don't you sit for a few minutes, until the waves chase us away?" He gestured to the sand beside him.

"I don't want to intrude."

Liar, liar. Why else did you come out here?

"You aren't. I was going to call you later, after I collected my thoughts. As long as you're here, maybe you can help me sort through them."

Was he just being polite?

No. Not based on the frustration—and confusion—in his voice.

She sat, leaving a discreet distance between them. For almost a full minute, Fletch gazed at the horizon as sand crabs scurried past, a dolphin crested the blue water in a graceful arc and gulls soared overhead.

Rachel kept a wary eye on the gulls.

"The woman you saw me with was Deke's wife."

Her attention snapped back to him. So he hadn't broken their date for a romantic rendezvous.

Relief washed over her, and the snarl of tension that had tightened her shoulders all afternoon began to unwind.

"She drove down from Savannah this morning. I had no idea she was coming until she called around eleven en route. I was actually at the grocery store getting a few snacks for this afternoon." Fletch turned toward her. "I'm sorry about the last-minute change of beach plans."

"We ended up here anyway."

"Yeah. But it's not quite the mood I had in mind."

What mood *had* he had in mind?

She kept that question to herself.

"The thing is, since Deke died I've tried to be available to her and David. Lately, I've been calling her a lot more than she calls me, so when she told me she was already on her way I figured something big was up."

"Was it?"

"Yeah." He lifted a handful of sand and watched the grains trickle through his fingers. "She's getting married again."

A few beats of silence ticked by while Rachel composed her response. "I take it that bothers you."

"It did, at first. Now…I don't know. A lot of what she said makes sense. She's dealt with her grief and guilt about dividing her loyalties, and she's at peace with her decision to move forward." He blew out a breath, picked up a shell from the small pile beside him and hurled it into the sea, watching it disappear under the waves. "I envy her that."

Pressure built in Rachel's throat. She tried to swallow past it, but her words still came out ragged. "I do, too."

He angled toward her. After a few moments, he removed his dark glasses. "I have a feeling there's a story behind that comment."

Now it was her turn to look away, toward the far-off horizon. She wasn't surprised he'd picked up on the significance of those three words…or noticed the catch in her voice. This was not a man who missed much.

But was she ready to share with him the shame she carried, as he'd shared his with her? His story was different, after all. His blame was misplaced. He'd done everything he was supposed to do in the life-and-death situation he'd faced. The choice had been horrendous: kill or possibly be killed. He'd had mere heartbeats to decide, and no opportunity to gather critical data. Anyone could make the wrong call under those circumstances.

She had none of those excuses.

The water crept closer. She studied the frothy bubbles and the undulating pattern of dark and wet sand the retreating wave left in its wake. Seconds later, the slate was wiped clean by a new breaker and a different pattern emerged.

Too bad it wasn't as easy to wash away guilt and start fresh.

Fletch broke the lengthening silence. "I think we'd better move or we'll end our afternoon with a rock-climbing excursion."

At his comment, she checked on the stairs. Waves were lapping at the base. In minutes, the first couple of steps would be underwater.

She scrambled to her feet. "We can avoid getting wet if we hug the rocks and time this just right."

"Sounds like you've done this before."

"Twice, when I got distracted and was caught unaware."

Fletch gestured for her to precede him. "I'll follow your lead."

She worked her way toward the stairs, watching the waves, waiting for one that would give them an opening to dash across the final stretch of wet sand and clamber up before the next one hit. Once they made the plunge, they'd have to forge ahead. There could be no looking back, no retreating.

It was the same thing she'd have to do if she opened her heart to Fletch.

And that might take more courage than she could muster.

But maybe…just maybe…with God's help she could manage it.

Fletch took a flying leap onto the step below Rachel as a wave crashed at his heels. "Made it. Good call on the timing."

"Too close for comfort, though." Grasping the railing, she began to ascend toward the long bridge that led over the dunes.

Fletch followed in silence.

She wasn't going to tell him her story.

Disappointment settled over him, weighing him down like the sixty pounds of gear he used to tote on his recon missions. Not that he needed any more angst today, but he'd hoped she'd feel comfortable opening up to him, trust him to listen without judging.

Then again, he hadn't done such a hot job of that with Lisa.

Maybe Rachel was wise to keep her secrets to herself.

Fletch continued his ascent, one step after the other, the steep climb taxing him far more than it would have if he'd had two real legs. Some days, keeping up the physical appearance of normalcy was almost as hard as maintaining the in-control emotional facade he presented to the world.

Almost.

In front of him, Rachel reached the top of the stairs. But instead of continuing over the long bridge, she turned and looked out across the sea.

He crested the last step and stopped beside her. Stairs might be more challenging in this post-SEAL life of his, but at least his rigorous daily exercise regime produced results. He wasn't even breathing heavily. An accomplishment he'd once taken for granted—like so much else.

"It's beautiful here, isn't it? Peaceful."

"Yeah." Fletch rested his hand on the railing, waiting for her to swivel around and cross the bridge over the dunes.

Instead, she gripped her arms over her chest, moistened her lips and swallowed.

He might have learned a lot about body language during his SEAL days, but a guy would have to be unconscious to miss the kind of stress signals Rachel was telegraphing. Waves of tension radiated from her, and her taut posture reminded him of a deer poised to leap over a chasm.

Every protective instinct in his body prodded him to take her hand. But would his touch encourage her to continue—or spook her into silence?

No way to know...and he couldn't take the risk. He wanted to hear her story.

So he waited, motionless, as five seconds ticked by. Ten. Fifteen.

When Rachel finally spoke, he started breathing again.

"I came here the summer after Mark died." Her throat worked, and as he adjusted his position a fraction to get a better view of her face, he caught the shimmer of tears in her eyes. "Just two weeks after I lost my baby."

For the second time in a handful of hours, he felt as if he'd been sucker punched.

Rachel was the mother of a child who had died?

The blindsiding revelations of the past few hours were leaving him as shell-shocked as the explosion on that mountain night in Afghanistan.

"I had no idea." Replies didn't get much more pathetic than that, but it was the best he could come up with while he was still reeling.

"Not many people do." Rachel brushed some sand off the railing and slanted him a quick glance. "Are you in a hurry?"

"No."

"We could sit here for a few minutes and watch the tide come in."

"Okay."

She lowered herself to the top step, and he joined her. Fortunately, the bridge and the stairs were wide enough for two people—but the arrangement was still cozy.

That suited him fine.

By the time they settled in, he'd had a chance to gather his wits and string some coherent words together. "I'm sorry, Rachel. I can't imagine losing both a spouse and a child. I have no idea how a person survives a tragedy like that."

He wanted to ask more. Wanted to know why, beneath her understandable grief, she also seemed troubled—and guilt-ridden. He, of all people, knew what those shadows in her eyes meant. He'd stared at them in his mirror every single day since Deke died.

But he couldn't risk pushing…and perhaps pushing her away. The implied question in his final comment left the door open for further discussion, putting the ball in her court. That was all he could do.

A single tear slid down her cheek, and she averted her face, scrubbing it away with her knuckles.

"It's even harder when…when it's all your fault."

At her broken words, his throat tightened, denial ricocheting through him. "I don't believe that."

Rachel took an unsteady breath and hunched forward, fists clenched in her lap. "Believe it."

"No."

Her head jerked toward him.

Fletch locked on to her gaze and held fast. "The Rachel who's working on a vacation home for the less fortunate, who got teary-eyed over a forlorn little girl she didn't know, who listened with compassion to the tale of a traumatized soldier, would never be a party to pain—or death."

Another tear formed and clung to a spiky lash. "Not on purpose." Her words came out in a whisper. "But pain or death that results from negligence and self-absorption makes you just as culpable."

Negligence and self-absorption?

Neither trait fit the woman sitting inches away from him.

A wave crashed into the base of the steps, sending spray flying, and Fletch tasted salt as he watched another tear trickle down Rachel's cheek. Tossing aside his SEAL-bred tendency to analyze every move, he reached over and wiped it away with the gentle pressure of his thumb. Then he folded her taut fingers in his hand. He could refute her words all he wanted, but she believed them. He needed to hear more before making his case.

"Do you want to tell me what happened?"

She looked down at their connected hands and released a shuddering sigh. "It's not a happy story."

"Neither was mine."

Lifting her chin, she studied him. "I thought the plan was to talk about the issues you wanted to sort through."

"We can get to that later."

After a moment, she refocused on the churning waves a few feet below them. The wind tugged a wisp of hair loose from her braid, and he was tempted to smooth it down, tuck it back in.

But once she began to speak, his attention shifted to her pain-etched words.

"I already told you about Mark's cancer. What I didn't tell you was that it would have been curable if we'd caught it earlier. It all started with a mole on the back of his leg that he'd had for years. I still can't believe such a small, innocent-looking thing could turn out to be so deadly."

The very same reaction he'd had to the small, innocent-looking children in Afghanistan.

Rachel continued as if she didn't expect him to respond. "He couldn't see it, but I could. I was just too focused on monitoring my own body, trying to pin down the perfect window for conception, to notice that the mole was changing shape and color. Once I did get pregnant, I was even more self-absorbed." Her chin quivered and she swallowed again. "A buddy from his gym spotted it a month after we toasted our upcoming parenthood."

Fletch did some quick math. Rachel had told him her husband only lived three months after the diagnosis. One month before that, her pregnancy had been confirmed.

Her husband had died while she was pregnant— and then she'd lost her baby, too.

A muscle in his jaw spasmed, and he closed his eyes.

Why, God?

It was the same question he'd flung at the Almighty over and over again while he was flat on his back at Landstuhl. While he grappled to accept that certain doors had closed forever. While he struggled to learn how to walk again. While he held a sobbing Lisa when she'd visited him in stateside rehab.

But God was as silent now as He had been then.

Rachel lifted her gaze from the churning waters and looked over at him, her eyes green pools of misery. "It gets worse."

Fletch gripped the edge of the step with his free hand and gave her fingers a gentle squeeze. "Tell me."

Her throat contracted, and she sniffed. "Mark died in early May. Three weeks later, on a rainy night, I rear-ended a car on my way home from the grocery store. It wasn't much more than a fender bender. The air bag didn't even deploy. But a couple of days later, I began to feel bad. By the time I went to the doctor, I'd been bleeding internally for two days." She fished in her pocket for a tissue. "Have you ever heard of placenta abruption?"

"No."

"Neither had I." Her breath was coming in ragged puffs now. "But that's what I had. The doctor told me if I'd gotten…medical attention after the accident, I might not…have miscarried. But I was so mired in grief and guilt over Mark's death…I didn't stop to think about the effect of the accident on my baby. I was self-absorbed—again. And it had fatal c-consequences—again." Rachel choked out the last few words between sobs, tissue wadded in her fingers, head bent.

Fletch could think of a lot of things to say in response to her litany of shortcomings and her claims of culpability—but those would keep. Right now, she needed touching more than talking.

Erasing the distance between them, he put his arm around her hunched shoulders and tugged her close, hoping she wouldn't resist.

She didn't.

Instead, she nestled into his chest, cheek resting near his heart, wisps of hair from her braid brushing his jaw, the faint scent of…jasmine?…wafting upward.

A shudder rippled through her, and then quiet sobs began to wrack her slim frame. They went on long enough to suggest she'd been holding her tears inside for weeks…months…years? And that wasn't healthy, according to the army shrink who'd visited him in the hospital. What had the man said? Something about how it was important to feel and release emotions rather than bury or bottle them.

At the time, he'd blown the guy off. Told him to get lost in language that could still make him cringe.

But the man might have had a point. Since he'd spilled his guts to Rachel at Francis House, under that jasmine vine, he'd felt better. The fact that she'd listened to his confession with empathy and kindness had comforted him more than he could ever have imagined.

Perhaps he could do the same for her.

When her sobs at last tapered off, she unclenched the wadded-up tissue from her fingers and dabbed at her eyes. "Sorry about that."

"No need to apologize. Turnabout is fair play. I dumped a lot on you that night at Francis House."

She eased away, and Fletch was tempted to tighten his grip, keep her within the circle of his arms. But he needed to let her call the shots on how the rest of this played out.

"You didn't cry all over my shirt." She summoned up a watery smile.

True.

But he'd been crying on the inside.

"SEALs don't cry."

Another tear leaked out of her eye, and she swiped it away. "For the record, I haven't cried like this in more than two years."

Fletch clasped his hands between his knees. "Also for the record, there's nothing wrong with crying. It's a healthy release—or so the shrinks told me when I was in the hospital."

"But you didn't."

"No."

"Ever?"

Did the stinging in his eyes during the endless, frustrating, excruciating physical-therapy sessions count? What about the way his vision had blurred when he'd visited Deke's grave with Lisa? Or the countless times he'd lingered in that suspended state between sleeping and wakefulness, lamenting that his life would never be the same, only to awaken and discover a damp pillow?

"If you have to think about it for that long, the answer is no."

He didn't dispute her.

Rachel pulled her legs up and hugged her knees. "Thank you for the sympathetic ear—even if I don't deserve it."

That was his cue.

"Did Mark blame you for what happened to him?"

She frowned. "No, of course not. He wasn't like that."

"Would you have blamed him if the situation had been reversed?" It was the same question Lisa had asked him about Deke…and if it had helped alter his perspective a tad, perhaps it would help Rachel.

Frustration tightened her features. "Look…I know what you're trying to do. But it won't work. I get that nobody's perfect. We all have our faults and make mistakes, and we're all called to forgive. I can do that with other people. Not so well with myself."

Fletch considered how best to proceed. "Where exactly was the mole?"

"Here." She pointed to a place on the back of her leg, closer to her hip than her knee.

"And you discovered it in February?"

"No, his gym buddy did. They liked one-on-one basketball. He spotted it on the court while they were playing."

"So Mark was wearing shorts?"

"Yes. He always did when he played basketball."

"But not at home?"

"Not at that time of year."

"Meaning in the winter you didn't often get a clear look at his leg in the kind of bright lights they have at gyms."

Rachel unclasped her arms from around her knees and rested her hands on top, her expression pensive. "No. I guess not."

"So the season may be as much to blame as you are."

"I don't know..." She shook her head, but he could tell she was thinking about it.

Good.

If nothing else, he'd planted a seed of doubt on one score.

Could he do the same with her guilt over her unborn child?

"I think there are also a lot of reasons not to blame yourself about the baby."

Her fingers tightened into fists, and she stiffened. He'd already pushed hard. Maybe too hard. But this wasn't the time to get cold feet, despite the back-off message her body language was sending.

Once more he covered one of her hands with his. "Don't shut me out, okay? Will you stay with me for a few more minutes?"

She exhaled…then nodded.

"Before that fender bender, you'd never heard of placenta abruption. Did the idea of seeking medical attention even cross your mind?"

"No. It wasn't that hard of a bump. But after Mark was diagnosed, I stopped reading my baby books. If I hadn't, I might have found out about potential problems like that. Maybe if I hadn't rescheduled my doctor's appointment to the next week he might have raised my awareness of the danger of jolts and bumps before I had the accident."

"That's a lot of ifs, mights and maybes."

Rachel regarded his hand covering hers. "Some days it seems that's the story of life." She looked over at him, her jade eyes dark with the pain of regret and loss. "I should also have been paying more attention to my driving. I never told this to anyone else, but right before the accident, I started to cry. The tears blurred my vision, and visibility was already bad because of the rain. I didn't notice the brake lights in front of me until it was too late. I shouldn't have kept driving while I was crying."

"You'd just lost your husband, Rachel. I doubt you were thinking straight. Cut yourself some slack."

"You didn't."

Touché.

But he'd learned a thing or two today.

"Can I ask you one more question?"

"I guess." Her tone was guarded.

"Was your husband a happy person?"

She seemed taken aback by the query, but she answered. "Yes. Very."

"So was Deke, as Lisa reminded me today. She said it wasn't fair to his memory for the two of us to spend the rest of our lives mourning. That while yesterday is written in stone and unchangeable, we can shape our tomorrows. And we can choose to honor the memory of those we loved by following their example and living every day with joy. She also told me to give my guilt to God and move on. I spent some time on the beach today trying to do that."

Rachel shifted toward him. "Did you succeed?"

"Let's just say the lines of communication are open again. It's a start."

"I'm glad for you."

A crane swooped low over the water in front of them, then dived. A few seconds later it flapped back into the sky with a fish in its bill, mission accomplished.

If only it were that easy to spot what you needed and retrieve it.

"I asked you once about the role faith played in your life." Rachel spoke slowly, tilting her head back to watch the crane soar against the sky. "You know I go to church every week with Aunt El, but the truth is, my faith took a major hit three years ago. Even though I want to do what your friend's wife said and give my guilt to God, I've never been able to manage it."

"Maybe that's why people say faith is a journey, not a destination."

"Maybe." The wind whipped some stray strands of hair across her face, and she brushed them back, gesturing toward the gray clouds cresting the horizon. "We may be in for a storm. Can I give you a ride back to your car?"

The sharing of confidences was over for today—but her willingness to trust him with her secrets had opened doors he intended to walk through in the tomorrows to come.

"Thanks. I'd appreciate it." He released her hand and rose.

She stood, too. "We never did talk about your stuff. I was supposed to help you sort through your thoughts."

"You did. A lot of Lisa's insights were relevant to your situation, and that helped me see how they might apply to mine."

Skepticism narrowed her eyes. "Are you being honest?"

"Always." Fletch took her arm and urged her across the bridge. "So about our missed lunch…we need to reschedule."

"I've got a class at the hotel tomorrow morning,

and I promised to help out at the Painted Pelican again in the afternoon. We're both on Francis House duty tomorrow night."

He expelled a breath. "That knocks tomorrow out. On Friday, I have to take Gram to Brunswick for a doctor's appointment, plus a physical-therapy evaluation. She also roped me into hauling some furniture to Francis House on Friday night."

Rachel descended the steps and gestured to the right, where her car was parked two doors down in front of a contemporary-style house. "Seems like fate is conspiring against us."

"Sometimes you have to take fate into your own hands." He followed her to the Focus.

"Easier said than done, given our commitments." She pulled her keys out of the pocket of her shorts and unlocked the car.

Fletch held her door, then circled around and slid into the passenger seat. "How does Saturday look?"

"So far, so good."

"Why don't we plan on dinner that night? We can talk specifics while we paint tomorrow."

As she swung out of her parking place and drove down the short street to the main road, her brow crinkled.

"What's with the frown?" Might as well address head-on the unsettled vibes he was picking up.

She kept her attention on the road as a few beats passed. "I still have issues to work through."

"So do I. One of them is you."

She flashed him a quick look but didn't respond.

"In case you haven't noticed, there is some serious electricity sparking between us."

Rachel flexed her hands on the wheel but didn't turn toward him. "I noticed."

"We need to get a handle on that. And the only way to do that is spend time together despite the loose ends in other parts of our life."

"I agree. That's why I was looking forward to our afternoon at the beach. But that seemed more casual somehow than a dinner date."

Hmm. In spite of all the personal information they'd shared, she wasn't yet ready to embrace the notion of a more serious, nighttime date.

Fine. He could deal with that…even if their time on the island was ticking by far too fast.

"We can switch it to Saturday afternoon if that makes you more comfortable. Same setup as today."

Rachel pulled into Fins and stopped beside his SUV. "Thanks for being so understanding."

He hitched up one side of his mouth. "You forgot 'patient.'"

"That, too."

"A SEAL trademark. Missions can depend on it."

Rachel leaned over to adjust the air conditioner, and another faint whiff of a familiar scent wafted his way.

"Is that jasmine?"

She fiddled with the dials as her cheeks pinkened. "Yes." Straightening up, she hesitated, then dug into the pocket of her blouse and extracted some limp leaves with a few curled-up brown globs attached that may, at one time, have been flowers. "It's from the night we talked on the porch at Francis House. I've been carrying a piece around with me ever since. I love the smell."

That might be true.

But her rosy cheeks told him her reason for carrying it around was a lot more personal than a fondness for jasmine's perfumelike fragrance.

And as Fletch watched her drive off a few moments later, he suddenly felt far lighter of heart than he had mere hours ago at this very restaurant.

Because Rachel was ready for romance.

She just didn't know it yet.

Chapter Eleven

"I wasn't sure why I kept all this stuff when I moved from Cincinnati, but now I see God had another use in mind for it." Eleanor dug deeper into the box in her third-bedroom-turned-attic and pulled out a lamp with a delft-patterned ceramic base. "Won't this look lovely in the living room at Francis House? All it needs is a shade."

Rachel gave it a once-over as she continued to sort through a carton of kitchen supplies at the other end of the room. "I saw one in the closet that might work."

"That's right. I did stash a few extras on the upper shelf." Eleanor set the lamp beside a brass headboard and wicker nightstand also destined for the renovated house and crossed to the closet. "By the way, did you have a nice afternoon with Fletch?"

Rachel gaped at her aunt's back.

How in the world…?

As if reading her mind, Aunt El swiveled toward her, lampshade in hand. "I saw you and Fletch pass by while I was waiting to turn onto Beachview on my way home from the shop. You seemed to be having a very intense discussion."

Doing her best to ignore the twinkle in Eleanor's eyes, Rachel kept her voice neutral. "We kind of ran into each other. It wasn't anything planned."

"How nice." Eleanor beamed at her. "Impromptu dates are often the best kind."

"It wasn't a date."

"It could be the next time, if you gave the man a little encouragement." Eleanor added the shade to her cache on the floor and planted her hands on her hips. "You're a very attractive young woman with a lot to offer, and Fletch is smart enough to recognize that."

"I told you, I'm not…"

"Stop." Aunt El held up her hand. "I don't want to hear that I-didn't-come-to-Jekyll-Island-for-romance speech again. I believe you. But sometimes love comes when we least expect it. You should be grateful Fletch is interested—and available."

The sudden hint of regret in her aunt's tone caught Rachel's attention. Did it have anything to do with that remark she'd made three weeks ago, about wishing she'd had the chance to marry and create a family?

Retrieving the extra toaster from the box in front of her, Rachel considered her strategy. Aunt El had retreated when she'd asked questions the last time this subject had come up—but might she be more receptive to discussing it today?

Maybe…if she eased into it by talking about her own situation.

She added the toaster to the pile of kitchen gadgets she'd assembled, then sat back on her heels. "I still love Mark, Aunt El. It's hard to let go."

For once, the other woman's usually sunny demeanor was melancholy. "I know."

Silence fell, and from the spot he'd claimed against the wall to watch the proceedings, Bandit lifted his head from his paws and looked back and forth between the two women as if to say, "What's up?"

Good question.

Based on Eleanor's expression, however, Rachel wasn't at all certain she was going to satisfy their curiosity.

She held her breath—and didn't let it out until the indecision faded from her aunt's eyes and she stood. "Follow me."

Together, Rachel and Bandit rose.

With the golden retriever close on her heels, Eleanor led the way to her bedroom and gestured toward the bed. "Have a seat."

As Rachel complied, Aunt El moved to her dresser, opened the top drawer and pulled out a white box with yellowed edges. When she sat on the bed, Bandit edged closer and settled in at her feet, as if sensing she might need comforting.

Eleanor took off the lid, a visible tremor quivering her hands.

A shock wave rippled through Rachel.

Aunt El was the most rock-solid woman she'd ever met. Nothing—and no one—ever flustered her. Yet whatever was in that old box still had the power to rattle her.

For a moment, Eleanor hesitated. Then, emitting a tiny puff of air, she pulled out a laminated black-and-white head shot from a newspaper and handed it over.

Rachel angled the photo toward the light coming in from the window behind her and studied the handsome man in the picture. He looked to be in his early forties, with dark hair and clear, direct eyes. Based on the cut of his lapels, the width of his tie and his hairstyle, the photo had to be close to fifty years old.

"That's Robert." Warmth and tenderness underscored the older woman's poignant tone. "The man I loved."

What?

The woman everyone in the family had pegged as a stereotypical spinster, who had either sidestepped romance and remained single by choice or had never met the right man, had once been head-over-heels in love?

Yet she'd never married.

Why?

As she pondered that question, Eleanor reached back into the box and withdrew a few more items, carefully setting each one on the bed between them. A matchbook from a restaurant named Pierre's. A few sheets of notepaper, tied with ribbon. Three birthday cards. A dried-up rose preserved in a Ziploc bag. A simple gold necklace with a sparkling blue stone on the end that looked like a sapphire.

"I was twenty-eight when I met Robert." Eleanor touched the faded ribbon on the notepaper. "He was forty. I'd never believed in love at first sight, but the day he joined my firm and the boss introduced us, I sensed he was different from any man I'd ever met. As I got to know him, that impression was confirmed. He was smart and kind and witty, and that smile of his…oh, my. He could dazzle you with that smile."

As Aunt El's own lips curved up in remembrance, Rachel examined the photo again. He did have a nice smile. And based on her aunt's sentimental collection of gifts and correspondence, he must have had feelings for her.

So what had gone wrong?

"Was the age difference a problem?"

At her tentative question, Eleanor sighed. "No, the problem was far more serious than that." She picked up the dead flower and cradled it in her hands. "Robert was married."

Rachel's jaw dropped. "You were involved with a married man?"

As the shocked, accusatory words reverberated in the small room, heat flooded her face. "I'm sorry. I didn't mean that to come out the way it sounded."

The older woman patted her knee. "No need to apologize. Your reaction shows your mother and father did a fine job raising you. Getting involved with a married man is, indeed, scandalous. That's why our relationship never became more than a friendship. To his credit, in the three years I knew Robert, he never once mentioned the word *love*."

Rachel frowned and gazed again at her aunt's meager treasure trove. It wasn't much to show for a three-year friendship, let alone a romance. "Then how did you know he had those kinds of feelings for you?"

"Ah, my dear." Eleanor's wistful expression tugged at her heart. "When someone cares about you in that way, you can see it in his eyes."

Rachel couldn't argue with that. It had been true between her and Mark…and she was picking up similar vibes from Fletch, despite their brief acquaintance. The electricity between them was potent. Surely the latter had more to do with hormones than hearts, though.

Didn't it?

But that was a question for another day.

Maybe.

Rachel refocused on her aunt. "So how did you two become friends?"

Eleanor set the rose back on the bed and picked up the matchbook. "It all began when Robert invited the women in my group to lunch to thank us for putting in extra hours on a priority project. As it turned out, we had heavy snow that day, and Robert and I were the only ones in the group who showed up for work. The two of us ended up going anyway, and things just clicked. After that, we often had lunch together. It was all very public and above-board. Robert was a man of honor and integrity."

The passage of years hadn't dimmed the light of love shining in Aunt El's eyes.

How tragic that the man who'd stolen her heart had already been committed to another.

"Did he ever talk about getting a divorce?" Rachel had a feeling she already knew the answer.

"No. He believed in his marriage vows. But the 'in sickness and in health' part was tested to the limits. His wife was an invalid. She had kidney disease, and many days she never even got out of bed. It wasn't much of a life for Robert, but he was clear from the beginning we could never be more than friends. Hence the yellow rose versus red." She touched the plastic bag. "Of course, his integrity only made me love him more. But as with most situations like this, things didn't end well."

"What happened?" Rachel leaned forward.

Bandit rested his chin on Aunt El's knee, and she gave him a gentle pat.

"Robert encouraged me to find someone who was free to marry. He didn't want me to end up alone. The trouble was, he'd spoiled me for everyone else. I tried dating other people—but there was no one like him…then, or in all the years since."

Eleanor picked up the necklace and weighed it in her hand. "He gave me this on my thirtieth birthday, along with the rose, and told me he thought we should stop having lunch. He said our friendship wasn't fair to me. The truth of it was, though, I lived for those lunches. It was the brightest spot in my week—and I suspect in his. So it didn't take much to convince him we should continue." Gently, Eleanor laid the necklace back on the bed. "And much as it shames me to admit this, I hoped if I hung in there, he might be mine after his wife died. That's awful, isn't it?"

Was it?

With all her own conflicted feelings surfacing in the past couple of weeks, who was she to say which feelings were right and which were wrong?

"I don't know, Aunt El. It wasn't as if you were hoping she would die."

"Close enough, I suppose." Eleanor shifted the blue stone in her fingers, watching it sparkle. "I always felt guilty about that. But in the end it didn't matter. A few weeks after my birthday lunch, Robert died at his desk of a massive heart attack."

As a second wave of shock rolled through Rachel and tears pricked her eyes, she took her aunt's hand. "I'm so sorry."

"Thank you, my dear." Aunt El let out a slow breath. "You know, I've wondered through the years if perhaps that was God's way of punishing me for morbidly waiting in the wings for someone to die—and for wanting a man I couldn't have."

"No." Rachel shook her head. "I had similar thoughts after I lost my baby, but that's wrong. God doesn't work that way."

"I know that up here." Eleanor tapped her temple. "But the mind and the heart don't always operate on the same wavelength." She picked up the ribbon-bound sheets of paper. "Robert left a letter for me with his lawyer—along with a key to a safe deposit box that contained a sizeable amount of money. They had no children, and his wife was well provided for, so he wanted to leave me some tangible evidence of his feelings. I invested wisely, and his bequest bought me this home."

"What happened to his wife?"

"I saw her death notice in the paper twelve years later."

So even if Robert had lived, Aunt El would have had to wait a long time for the man she loved.

Eleanor touched her arm. "I know what you're thinking, but good things in life are worth waiting—and sacrificing—for. However, I didn't tell you this story to make you sad. I told it to you because I want you to know I would have married after Robert died if I'd found the right man. When two people are in love they want the best for each other. And what could be better than spending your life with someone you love, raising a family together and growing old with your grandchildren all around you? If a man like Fletch had come into my life years ago, I might very well have married. He's the real deal. True hero material—both on and off the battlefield."

The focus had swung back to her and Fletch, just as Rachel had expected.

"Is that why you and Louise finagled to get us both here at the same time?"

Eleanor sent her a get-real look and began to stow her treasures back in the yellowed box. "Are you suggesting Louise broke her wrist on purpose to entice Fletch to come here so the two of you could meet?"

Put into words, it sounded silly.

"No, of course not."

"The timing turned out to be providential, that's all." Eleanor settled the lid on the box and stood, cradling it in her hands. "But if I were you, I wouldn't look a gift horse in the mouth. You may think you're not ready for romance, but opportunities to meet outstanding men don't come along every day. Most people are lucky if it happens once in a lifetime." She stroked a hand over the box, then crossed the room, deposited it in her dresser and closed the drawer.

"I'm just saying you should think long and hard before you pass up this chance. Is there any harm in getting to know him better?"

Two weeks ago, Rachel would have said yes—because Jack Fletcher was the kind of guy who could upend your world. Push you out of your comfort zone. Make you wish for things you didn't think you deserved.

Now, after the confidences they'd shared, after their conversation today, she was beginning to think his unexpected appearance in her life was more destiny than disaster.

"I can see you're thinking about it. You keep doing that…but don't dither too long, like your customer at the shop. Mrs. Gardner got her artwork before someone else grabbed it—but if you don't stake a claim, some other woman is going to come along and snatch Fletch right out from under your nose." Aunt El brushed off her hands and started toward the door. "Now, let's get back to the attic room and finish up. There's an old Bette Davis movie on cable tonight I want to catch."

Bandit fell in behind Aunt El as she exited the bedroom while Rachel followed more slowly.

Her aunt was right about one thing. Based on everything she'd seen so far, Fletch was the real deal—and while his rendezvous with Lisa today hadn't been romantic, one of these days soon some woman was going to steal his heart.

The sudden sinking feeling in the pit of her stomach…the very same one she'd experienced when she'd spotted that little tête-à-tête at Fins…was easy to identify.

It was jealousy, plain and simple.

Meaning like it or not, she was falling for Fletch.

But he wasn't going to hang around here a whole lot longer. In two or three weeks, max, he'd be heading north. And she wasn't a fast mover.

So where did that leave them?

Bandit paused at the attic room door and looked back at her, as if to say, "If you drag your feet you're going to get left behind."

An excellent point—and serious food for thought.

Fletch bit back a word he rarely used, jammed his phone into the holster on his belt and glared at the screen of his laptop.

"Trouble?" Gram came through the kitchen door and stopped on the threshold.

"Work problems. What are you doing up this late?"

"It's only ten-thirty. I was watching a cable movie in my room, but I'm about to turn in. What about you? Aren't you tired after spending the whole evening hauling furniture to Francis House?"

"More like aggravated after that last call."

"What's up? Or is this one of those classified jobs you can't talk about?"

"Without naming names, one of my clients just received a credible threat and has gone into lockdown mode. They want me on-site to supervise security until the threat's been neutralized. I need to fly out first thing tomorrow."

Before his afternoon date with Rachel.

At this rate, they were never going to get any time alone.

Gram tut-tutted. "Your clients certainly keep you hopping. Midnight conference calls, long hours, unexpected trips."

"That's the nature of this kind of work. Will you be okay while I'm gone?"

"Don't you worry about me. I'm learning to adapt to this thing around the house." She lifted her plaster-encased wrist. "And I can call Eleanor for a ride if I need to go anywhere. Besides, the doctor said today that I can ditch the cast in two weeks. Then you can go home and get on with your own life."

At one time, that would have been welcome news.

Now, since leaving the island also meant leaving Rachel, the prospect was far less appealing.

Gram opened the door of the fridge, extracted a soda and examined the white bags with the logo of the gourmet food shop he'd visited in Brunswick during her physical-therapy appointment.

"What about your date with Rachel?"

"It's not going to happen."

She shook her head and closed the refrigerator. "Such a shame. All that expensive food...maybe you can save some of it for the Fourth of July. You'll be back by then, won't you?"

"I hope so."

"You don't want to miss the holiday here. The fireworks are spectacular."

That was probably true…but he had a different kind of fireworks in mind, if all went well—an even bigger incentive to wrap up the trip ASAP.

"I'll do my best." He started checking flight times. "Why don't you eat the paté, though? I don't think that will last five days."

"Paté? My, you did go all out."

He let that pass as he perused the airline site for the next available flight. 6:30 a.m. out of Brunswick, with a connection in Atlanta, was the best he could do. That would put him on the ground with his client by noon.

Right about the time he was supposed to meet Rachel.

Once again, he bit back a word Gram wouldn't like.

When he didn't respond to her last comment, Gram tried again. "Rachel's a very nice girl."

He looked up. She was struggling with the tab on her soda can, and he rose to join her. "Yeah, she is. Here, let me." He tugged the can from her grip, pulled the tab and glanced at his watch as he handed it back. "Do you think it's too late to call Eleanor's house?"

"No. I know for a fact she was going to watch the same movie I did tonight, and I doubt a young woman like Rachel turns in this early on a Friday night." She rose on tiptoe and kissed his cheek. "Try to get to bed at a reasonable hour."

Given his client's emergency, that wasn't likely.

"I'll wrap this up as fast as I can. Sleep well."

"I'd sleep better if your date with Rachel tomorrow was still on."

So would he.

"Can't be helped. But I'll give her a call as soon as I book my flights for tomorrow and set up another date."

"In that case, I'll let you get to it. Will I see you in the morning?"

"No. I'll be long gone before sunrise."

"Then have a safe trip—and hurry back."

As she disappeared down the hall, he returned to his laptop and made his flight reservations. Once that was taken care of, he pulled his cell off his belt and exited onto the patio. In light of all the matchmaking shenanigans Gram and Eleanor had been pulling, he wouldn't put it past her to eavesdrop on his call.

Propping one shoulder against the edge of her morning-glory-covered pergola, Fletch waited while the phone rang three times. Just as he expected it to roll to voice mail, Rachel's breathless hello came over the line.

"Sorry to call so late. I hope you weren't sleeping."

"Fletch?" Surprise and a touch of—pleasure?—warmed her words. "No. I was still sorting through stuff for Francis House in Aunt El's attic room. What's up?"

"As much as I hate to do this, I'm afraid I'm going to have to cancel our date for tomorrow. One of my clients has an emergency and needs me on-site. I'm flying out at dawn."

She exhaled, making no attempt to hide her disappointment. He hoped that was a positive omen for their relationship. "There must be some kind of jinx against us getting together."

"I don't believe in jinxes—and SEALs are nothing if not tenacious. We don't let a few setbacks deter us from a mission. I'll be back by Tuesday if possible, but no later than Wednesday. I hear they have great fireworks here on the holiday…and I'm in the mood for fireworks."

A beat of silence ticked by, and a smile twitched at his lips. If she wanted to read more into his comments about missions and fireworks, he wasn't about to stop her.

"Maybe we can reschedule after you get back."

"No maybes about it. In fact, let's get something on the books now. Do you have any plans for the Fourth?"

"Last year, Aunt El and I went to the beach and got hamburgers and funnel cakes for dinner, then watched the fireworks. We haven't talked about it yet for this year, but I imagine we'll do the same thing and that your grandmother will join us."

He plucked a spent blossom off the morning glory vine and rolled it around in his fingers. If Rachel had been nervous about a dinner date alone with him, she might also object to a cozy twosome on the beach as they watched fireworks, even amidst a crowd. It might be more prudent to play this safe—at least for the early part of the evening.

"If that's their plan, why don't I join the party?"

Silence.

"Okay." She didn't sound all that thrilled about the notion of a group date.

That was encouraging.

"If I can get back sooner, I'll call you. Sorry to do this twice in a row."

"I understand. Duty calls. Besides, look on the bright side. You're off the hook from Francis House detail for a few days."

"There is that." He watched a doe poke her head out from the wooded area behind Gram's house and cautiously look around. "Think of me while you're painting."

"I'm on the curtain-hanging crew this week."

"Better you than me. Although I wouldn't mind juggling drapes if you were holding the other end. And I wouldn't mind sharing another soda on the front porch."

A car backfired nearby. The doe froze, then leaped back into the woods and vanished.

Careful, Fletch. You don't want that to happen with Rachel. Keep things nice and easy...for now.

When the silence between them lengthened, he spoke again. "I'll be in touch soon."

"Okay. Have a safe trip."

As they said their goodbyes, the clouds parted and the moon bathed the landscape in a silver glow. Once more the doe emerged from the woods, step by tentative step, ready to dart away again at the slightest hint of threat. Fletch remained motionless, and she finally relaxed enough to forage among the leaves and twigs along the perimeter of the woods.

One wrong move, though, and she'd bolt—just as Rachel would.

No way was he going to risk that. Yes, their time on the island was running out. Yes, he was inclined to accelerate things. But for once in his life, he didn't care if a woman was GU. Because geographically undesirable or not, Rachel was worth any effort required to continue this relationship after he returned to Norfolk.

And before he bid Gram goodbye, Fletch intended to do everything in his power to make sure Rachel felt the same way—even if that meant delaying a certain kind of fireworks long past the Fourth of July.

But if nothing else, he intended to test the waters come Wednesday.

Chapter Twelve

Fletch wasn't going to make it back for the Fourth of July.

As rain lashed across the picture window in Aunt El's sky room, Rachel watched the palm trees writhe in the wind. They didn't look at all happy to be in the midst of a tropical storm.

She could relate.

The hurricane forming off the Florida coast might not be headed directly toward Jekyll, but no planes would be landing or taking off at the Brunswick airport anytime soon. And since it was already four o'clock in the afternoon, the odds that things would change by tomorrow's holiday were nil.

"Rachel? Are you up there?"

At Aunt El's summons, she moved to the landing and looked over the railing. "Yes. Watching the storm."

"It's a doozy, that's for sure. I'm glad I closed the shop at three. Have you heard from Fletch?"

"No." Despite her attempt to maintain a neutral tone, the word came out in a dispirited sigh.

"Well, don't you fret. I imagine cell service is disrupted. As for the weather, I can't recall a Fourth of July where the Jekyll Island fireworks didn't go off as planned—and Fletch'll get back if he can, I guarantee it. You go ahead and watch Mother Nature throw her tantrum while I get dinner started."

As her aunt headed toward the kitchen, Rachel wandered back to the window. The beach where she and Fletch had first met—and later exchanged confidences—had disappeared beneath the churning, restless waves that were slamming against the huge boulders at the edge, sending spray flying.

Could her emotions of late find a more perfect metaphor than that turbulent sea? And all the blame rested on a certain SEAL who'd walked into her life and heated up her annual chill-out trip, awakening feelings and longings that had lain dormant for three long years.

Gaze on the horizon, Rachel pressed her forehead against the glass. The rain-streaked pane distorted the scene, much as grief and guilt had distorted her view of life for the past three years.

She moved back, and the scene sharpened.

Distance clarified—and restored perspective.

And after weeks of disrupted sleep, heavy-duty soul-searching, and fervent prayer, she was beginning to regain perspective and see more clearly. The storm outside might be raging, but the storm within was at last diminishing.

Because Deke's wife was right.

If you loved someone deeply, you wanted what was best for him or her. Had she been the one diagnosed with melanoma, she would have told Mark the same thing he'd told her—find someone new and love again. He would want her to create the family she'd always yearned for, not spend her life alone.

Now, out of the blue, a man who might offer her a second chance at that dream had come into her life—and as Aunt El had pointed out in no uncertain terms, she'd be a fool to pass up this unexpected opportunity.

So if Fletch began dropping hints about fireworks or pressing her for more dates once he came back, she wasn't going to shy away.

She was going to put her trust in God and see if this special man did, indeed, hold her future in his hands.

"Well, look who made it to the party after all!" Louise waved toward the parking area.

Shifting around on the picnic bench, Rachel took in the scene over her shoulder.

Fletch was weaving through the crowd in the beachside pavilion, heading straight for the two picnic tables Louise and Aunt El and several other members of their congregation had commandeered for the Fourth of July festivities.

The slow smile he aimed her direction tripped her pulse into double-time, and she groped for an empty paper plate to fan the sudden warmth in her cheeks.

As he joined them, everyone on her side of the picnic table scooted over to make room for him. Aunt El tugged her along, and he slid in beside her, his leg brushing hers.

A spurt of adrenaline buzzed through her.

He was close enough for her to get a whiff of his appealing aftershave.

Close enough to feel the heat emanating from his skin.

Close enough to see he was freshly shaved and that his hair was damp from a very recent shower.

She fanned harder.

"Have some lemonade, Fletch." Aunt El leaned across her and set a plastic cup in front of him.

"Thank you." He raised the cup in salute, then lifted it to his lips and took a long swallow, giving Rachel a heart-stopping view of his chiseled jaw and strong profile.

She tried not to stare.

"I was beginning to think you weren't going to make it." Louise rested her cast on the table. "I've been keeping watch for the past two hours."

As Louise's words registered, Rachel ripped her gaze away from Fletch and directed it toward the older woman. His grandmother had known he was on the way?

"I almost didn't." He set the lemonade down and angled toward her, his leg once more brushing hers. *Keep breathing, Rachel.* "That's why I didn't call you. I didn't want to make a promise I couldn't keep or raise false expectations. I got as far as Atlanta late yesterday afternoon, right before Brunswick shut down. I hung out at the airport, hoping things would improve, but nothing moved this direction again until three o'clock this afternoon."

"You spent twenty-four hours at the airport?" Rachel examined the shadows under his eyes and the fine lines at their corners. No wonder the man looked exhausted.

He shrugged. "I've had plenty of experience waiting in far less hospitable places for far less pleasant payoffs." Giving her a discreet nudge that played havoc with her respiration, he took another swig of lemonade. "I considered renting a car, but the weather reports started to sound promising so I decided to sit it out and hope for the best."

"Things improved dramatically once the wind shifted. I knew they would. Jekyll Island fireworks haven't been rained out once since I've lived here." Aunt El broke off a bite of funnel cake and shoved the grease-soaked paper plate toward Rachel. "I've eaten far more than my share. The rest is yours."

As Rachel inspected the pile of fried dough, Hank

appeared at the end of the table and slid a plate with a burger and a mound of coleslaw in front of Fletch. "Saw you coming as I made my way back from the gent's room so I took a detour. A man who's been on the road for over twenty-four hours needs to eat."

Rachel canvassed the table. Did everyone except her know Fletch had been on his way back?

"So how did everything go with that top-secret emergency of yours?" Louise reached across the table and broke off a piece of Rachel's funnel cake.

"Fine." Fletch spoke around a huge bite of burger, waiting until he swallowed to continue. "We put in a lot of long hours, but everything's back to normal now."

Aunt El sized him up. "No wonder you look tired. You should be catching up on shut-eye, not partying."

"On my agenda—after the fireworks." He stopped wolfing down his food long enough to give Rachel a subtle wink.

Another surge of heat warmed her cheeks, and she bent her head on the pretense of examining the remains of the funnel cake. While she might be open to exploring fireworks of a personal nature with Fletch, she'd rather keep that to herself until she had a better sense of whether this thing with him was going anywhere.

"You don't have long to wait. Another twenty minutes or so, tops." Once more, Louise leaned sideways and peered past Rachel, toward the parking lot. "Here come Reverend Carlson and Susan. Yoo hoo!" She waved her good hand in the air.

While Fletch demolished his burger, the minister stopped beside their table, arm in arm with his wife. "Happy Fourth of July to you all."

A murmur of best wishes rippled through the group while Susan surveyed the crowded pavilion. "I'm sorry I delayed us, Jim. The place is packed."

"The phone calls with the children were well worth a little hassle. We needed to finalize the plans for their visits. I'm sure we'll find somewhere to perch for the fireworks. If not, I can always run home and get a couple of folding chairs."

Fletch finished off his lemonade and leaned close to Rachel. "I have a blanket in the SUV. Want to find a spot on the beach and give the reverend and his wife our seats?"

Her heart skipped a beat.

A blanket on the beach with Fletch versus dealing with a sorrier-by-the-minute-looking funnel cake and listening to the octogenarians around her discuss Hank's upcoming knee replacement?

No contest.

"Sure."

Fletch slid off the bench, and Rachel scooted after him as he spoke. "Why don't you two take our seats? We're going down to the beach to watch the show."

"Are you certain you don't mind?" Reverend Carlson directed his question to both of them. "We don't want to evict you."

"Of course they don't mind." Susan promptly took Rachel's seat and patted the bench beside her. "I'm sure the young people would rather be closer to the action."

Rachel narrowed her eyes as the minister sat and Fletch headed for the parking lot with an "I'll be back in a minute" promise.

Was this a setup?

Louise and Aunt El and the minister's wife appeared to be the picture of innocence as they chatted about an upcoming book sale at the church—yet Fletch conveniently had a blanket in his Explorer.

At this point, though, who cared? She'd wanted fireworks; now she was going to get them. Despite the crowds on the beach, she had a feeling that given positive signals and the right opportunity, Fletch would find a way to set off some fireworks of his own before this night was over.

And she intended to make certain he got both.

"How's this?" Fletch gestured to a small unoccupied expanse of sand, giving the crowded beach a final annoyed scan. If a more secluded spot was available, he couldn't spot it the deepening dusk. Based on the crowd, everyone on the island—plus thousands of others—had turned out for the holiday display. Any fireworks of a personal nature would have to come after the official display ended.

"Fine. We'll have a perfect view from here." She grabbed an edge of the blanket as he shook it out, and together they spread it on the sand.

He waited until she settled in before dropping down beside her.

"So was this a setup?" She gestured to the blanket.

Fletch hesitated.

"I think that's my answer." She arched an eyebrow at him as she pulled her legs up and wrapped her arms around her knees.

He leaned back on his palms and crossed his ankles. Might as well be honest. "If you're asking me whether I knew exactly how the scene in the pavilion was going to play out, the answer is no. But Gram did suggest I throw a blanket in the Explorer in case the opportunity came up for me to invite you to watch the show on the beach."

"And she made sure it did."

"She and several others, I suspect."

"No kidding. I think they were all in on the plan."

"You could have turned down my offer."

She shrugged. "The minister and his wife needed a place to sit. Besides, coming to the beach with you gave me an excuse to walk away from a funnel cake I didn't want."

"Gee, thanks for the ego boost."

She sent him a wry look. "Give me a break. That

Navy SEAL mystique has to be a serious chick magnet. I don't think your ego is suffering."

Her flirty repartee was new—and encouraging.

"Yeah. I've had to beat the women off with a palm frond since I've been here. So is my 'mystique' one of the reasons you went along with my suggestion?" He leaned in close, until their eyes were only inches apart. If she could flirt, he could, too. "Or did the electricity come into play?"

Her lips parted slightly, and several seconds passed while a pulse throbbed in the hollow of her throat.

A sudden peal of children's laughter a few yards in front of them broke the mood, and she shifted that direction...leaving his question unanswered.

Remember, Fletcher. Slow and easy. Take it one step at a time.

Check.

He transferred his attention to the two youngsters, too. The boy appeared to be about six, the girl perhaps four. Despite the quickly fading light, they were still engrossed in building a sandcastle.

"That little girl is about to lose a flip-flop." Rachel stood and gestured to a bobbing, fluorescent pink object that had been snatched by the retreating surf. "I'll be right back."

She wove through the groups of people scattered on blankets, bent to snag the flip-flop and returned it to the little girl.

He watched as she chatted with the children, then

stayed to help them invert a bucket of sand and shore up the defensive wall of their castle. She returned a few minutes later, brushing the damp sand off her hands. "Sorry about that. Where kids are concerned, I tend to jump in headfirst and get way too involved."

"I already figured that out. Have you heard anything more from Madeleine's mother, by the way?"

"As a matter of fact, she dropped me a thank-you card a few days ago. I didn't do all that much, but I was glad to hear things are going well."

"So she's seen the light?"

"I think so." Rachel ran her palm over the sand, smoothing out the bumps, and her voice grew wistful. "I guess maybe for some women it takes a dramatic wake-up call like that to appreciate the gift of motherhood. But one of the happiest times of my life was while I was pregnant. Carrying a child conceived in love, feeling that new life move within you, close to your heart, knowing he or she is part of both of you—it was the most profound, joy-filled experience of my life."

As her passionate, emotion-choked words hung in the air between them, Fletch's stomach suddenly bottomed out.

He'd known Rachel loved children, of course. Had assumed she'd want a family if she ever remarried.

But until this moment, he hadn't realized how much she'd cherished carrying a baby she'd created with the man she loved.

And she deserved a second chance at that.

Rachel took a slow, deep breath and validated his conclusion. "Some women find pregnancy burdensome, but for me it was a precious blessing. One Mark and I had hoped to receive several times—until that dream died along with him."

A test rocket went up, exploded with a loud bang... and fizzled.

Just like his spirits.

Gritting his teeth, he clenched the blanket in his fingers. How could he have been so blind? He was a SEAL, trained to interpret data and observe subtle signals. He had no one to blame but himself for failing to recognize this looming disaster—and to realize the secret he'd hoped would be a mere disappointment was, in fact, a deal-breaker.

The whistle of a rocket pierced the air, and a few seconds later the sky exploded with color.

Rachel tipped her head back, and as the glow illuminated her face, catching the delicate curve of her jaw and the elegant line of her neck, he swallowed. Hard.

This night wasn't turning out anything close to the way he'd hoped.

The vibrant color faded, and as the sky went black again he felt her shift toward him in the darkness.

"By the way...the answer to your earlier questions is yes." Her voice was softer now—and endearingly shy. "Both the SEAL mystique and the electricity are appealing. But to be honest, the attraction is a whole lot deeper than that."

A shaft of pain pierced Fletch's midsection, so intense it stole the breath from his lungs. Was this some kind of cruel cosmic joke? First, Rachel opens a door by agreeing to share his blanket. Then she slams it shut with a game-changing revelation. Now she opens it again and invites him in.

But he couldn't accept. Encouraging her to fall in love with a man who wasn't able to give her the special joy she longed to experience again was selfish. As Lisa had reminded him, when you love someone, that person's happiness matters above all else. And if he wasn't already in love with the woman beside him, he was falling fast.

Another rocket exploded, lighting the night sky with a brilliant flash of stunning color. The next instant the radiant burst vanished, leaving the sky even darker than before.

Was that how his life would feel if he let Rachel walk away?

Yet what choice did he have?

She scooted a bit closer, until her elbows brushed his, issuing a clear invitation to drape his arm across her shoulder.

Ten minutes ago, Fletch would have taken full advantage of it.

But not now.

There would be no fireworks this night other than the ones in the sky above them.

The bitter taste of despair soured his mouth, and as desperation sent a wave of panic crashing over him, he did something he hadn't done in a very long while.

He prayed—for fortitude, guidance…and grace.

Because he was going to need all three in abundance in the days ahead.

Chapter Thirteen

Talk about a bust.

Paintbrush in hand, Rachel huffed out a breath and backed away to examine the whimsical dolphin mural in a children's bedroom at Francis House. Given how distracted she'd been since her dud date last night with Fletch at the fireworks display, it was a wonder she hadn't added a third eye to the frolicking critter.

What was with him, anyway?

First, he drops all kinds of clues that he's interested in romance. Then, when she gives him plenty of opportunities to get cozy, he retreats. Worse, he'd used fatigue to deflect her hints that she'd be receptive to a ride home. To cap it off, he hadn't said a word about getting in touch or rescheduling their beach date.

Even Aunt El and Louise had seemed taken aback by his behavior when they'd all parted for the night.

Sheesh.

She dipped her brush into the paint and attacked the wall again, creating a whitecap in the once-placid sea.

What could account for his sudden change of heart?

Yes, the man had been tired. She got that. From all indications, he'd put in some grueling days—and nights. But would a strapping former Navy SEAL ever be too tired for romance…especially a romance he'd been pursuing with dogged diligence?

With a sharp twist of her wrist, Rachel created yet another churn in the water. She'd gone over and over that question into the wee hours of the morning, and the answer was always the same.

No.

Fletch wasn't the kind of man who backed away from a mission. And if that mission was a woman, he might be judicious and tactical in his approach, but he'd keep advancing—no matter how exhausted he was.

Instead, he appeared to be in full retreat.

And men thought women were hard to figure out!

At least she'd had her art class at the hotel to keep her busy this morning and the mural project she'd started over the weekend to occupy her afternoon.

Too bad neither had been mentally demanding enough to keep thoughts of a certain security consultant at bay.

Once more she stepped back to examine her work.

Another hour and she ought to be able to wrap it up. If nothing else, things at Francis House had progressed well in the past few days. Aside from a few decorating details, it would be ready for the Mitchell family's arrival and ribbon-cutting in nine…

A glint at the front window—like sun reflecting off metal—caught her eye, and she wandered over to investigate.

Was that Fletch's SUV parked in front?

She edged closer, approaching from the side, and peeked through the blinds.

It was his, all right. The man himself was sitting in the driver's seat.

Rachel squinted, trying to figure out what he was doing, but the light was against her. All she could tell for sure was that his hands were clasped on the wheel.

Had he come looking for her?

But no one knew about her impromptu trip except Aunt El. Nor did anyone except her aunt know she was here alone, since Eleanor had made a last-minute decision to dispatch today's Francis House crew to round up paper goods and basic cooking supplies for the kitchen.

Of course, Aunt El could have called Louise from the Painted Pelican—and Louise could have told Fletch.

But given his lack of interest last night, why would he seek her out?

As she watched his motionless figure, a tiny shiver snaked up her spine. Fletch was a decisive man of action, yet his frozen posture suggested he was waging some sort of internal debate as he sat there in the afternoon heat.

Her fingers tightened on the paintbrush as fear congealed in her throat. Was he summoning up the courage to break things off with her face-to-face?

Based on his sudden withdrawal in the middle of what had started out to be a promising evening last night, that was a very real possibility.

Foreboding wrapped itself around her like the tentacles of an octopus, and she retreated into the shadows.

One thing for sure. Something was up—and it wasn't good.

His knuckles were turning white.

Prying his hands off the steering wheel, Fletch flexed his fingers until the blood began flowing again.

Too bad it wasn't that easy to alleviate the constriction around his heart.

He glanced toward Francis House. If only he could drive away and pretend he'd never met Rachel. Or better yet, find a way to eliminate the problem that was dooming their relationship.

But since neither was possible, he might as well get this over with. Besides, he owed her an explanation for his mixed signals last night. The image of her hurt, confused face when he'd begged off driving her home had strobed across his mind through the lonely, dark, endless hours of the night.

It had been on Gram's mind, too, this morning, based on her pithy comments during breakfast about consideration and manners and people whose heads weren't on straight.

He needed to make things right—or as right as he could under the circumstances.

Expelling a slow breath, he opened the door, stepped into the sun and braced for what was sure to be one of the hardest conversations he'd ever had.

As he approached the porch, he eyed the swing, now sporting a padded seat. The house was almost ready to welcome its first family for a relaxing visit to one of Georgia's Golden Isles.

He hoped their stay was less problem-plagued than his.

Clenching his left hand into a fist, he stabbed the bell with his right index finger.

The door opened at once, as if Rachel had been hovering on the other side. She had a small brush in her hand, and there was a speck of blue paint on her nose.

She looked adorable—but wary.

After last night's debacle, that didn't surprise him.

"I thought you'd moved on to curtains." He gestured to the brush.

She looked down, as if she'd forgotten it was in her hand. "Oh. We…uh…finished hanging them on Sunday. I decided to do a mural in one of the bedrooms." She gestured vaguely behind her with the brush.

"May I see it?" That was as expedient a way as any to get into the house.

She sent him a quizzical glance, then lifted one shoulder. "Sure." Pulling the door wide, she moved aside to allow him to enter. "It's the blue room."

A dozen steps took him to the threshold, and despite the knot in his stomach his lips curved up at the fanciful image of two dolphins cavorting in the waves with a beach ball. "Nice."

"It's not the kind of painting I usually do while I'm here. I tend to dabble more in impressionistic seascapes. But I think the younger visitors to Francis House will enjoy it."

They were back on the subject of children again.

The very opening he needed—ready or not.

Just do it, Fletcher.

Forcing himself to turn, he faced her across the room. "I want to apologize for last night."

Rachel's cheeks pinkened, and she eased back toward the far wall, snatched up a rag and busied herself wiping specks of paint off her hands. "You didn't do anything wrong."

"I didn't do anything right, either."

She flashed him a look but remained silent.

Raking the fingers of one hand through his hair,

Fletch propped the other on his hip. "Just so you know, I had every intention of initiating some fireworks of our own last night. You didn't misread my signals—and it took every ounce of my self-control to ignore yours."

For a couple of seconds she studied him, as if debating how to respond. Finally, she swallowed and wadded the rag in her fingers. "So why did you?"

At least she hadn't taken the face-saving route and denied her interest. That would have made things even more awkward—if that was possible.

"It's a long and unpleasant story. Would you like to sit outside on the porch swing for a few minutes while I tell it to you? That jasmine vine smells a whole lot better than this paint." He tried to coax his lips into a smile, but they refused to cooperate.

After a fractional hesitation, she tossed the rag onto the tarp covering the floor. "Okay."

While he followed her back to the front door, Fletch reconsidered the speech he'd formulated last night during the long hours before dawn chased away the darkness. In the light of day, it seemed somehow stilted and much too cold and clinical. That wasn't the mood he wanted to create with this lovely, vibrant woman, even if their relationship—such as it was—was destined to be short-lived.

Maybe he'd wing it…and hope God provided the right words when he needed them.

Rachel pushed through the door and led the way to

the swing. He sat beside her and set it moving with a prod of his foot. The fragrance of the jasmine wafted their way, and he inhaled the scent, wishing it could sweeten the words he had to say.

Since that wasn't going to happen, he gritted his teeth, angled toward her and plunged in. "I don't think I've made any secret of the fact I thought our relationship had serious potential."

Rachel swallowed, her gaze locked with his. "No."

"But I neglected to pass on some information I now realize is a deal-breaker."

Rachel scrutinized his face, but she waited in silence for him to continue.

"I told you about the night I lost my foot. I also mentioned I'd suffered blunt-force trauma to my chest and abdomen. What I didn't tell you was that the trauma had permanent repercussions." He braced, then forced himself to continue, his heart hammering as hard as it once had in explosive combat situations. "To keep this as simple and delicate as possible, while I'm functional in every way, I sustained some serious damage to my ductwork. I can never father a child. No woman will ever carry my baby."

In the silence that followed, Fletch watched Rachel absorb his news. It took her a mere handful of seconds—three or four, tops—but in those few beats, a parade of emotions whooshed across her face. Comprehension. Shock. Compassion. Sorrow. And then a slight shutting down...and a subtle withdrawal.

It was the latter that doomed him, confirming that his news was, indeed, a deal-breaker.

Because no matter what she might say now, no matter how she might try to find an answer for them short of severing their relationship, her expression hadn't lied in those first few, honest moments.

The tiny spark of hope in his heart that had refused to die flickered and went out.

Rachel reached over and covered his fisted hand with hers. "I'm sorry, Fletch."

"So am I." The words came out raspy, and he cleared his throat.

"Are you absolutely certain about this?"

"Yeah. I've been checked and rechecked. If I could have gotten medical attention in the first hour, things might have been different. Given the circumstances, however, I was lucky to escape with my life."

"Still...that doesn't mean you can't have a family."

"No. There are a lot of options these days for people who want children. But I watched you when you talked about being pregnant, and I understand how much that meant to you. I can't give you that—and you deserve another chance to create a child with the man you love."

Rachel rubbed her temple. Ran a finger over the links in the chain that held up the swing. "Maybe that's not the most important thing in the end."

Her comment was more question than statement—
once again affirming his decision to back off.

"Rachel." He captured her fingers, urging her to
look at him. "Can you honestly tell me you won't
care if you never carry another child conceived with
the man you love?"

The flicker of doubt in her eyes gave him her answer before she spoke. "I—I don't know. I need to
think about it. This just…it came out of the blue. It
isn't a choice I thought I'd ever have to face."

"And you don't need to face it now." Fletch released her hand and forced himself to stand, to move
toward the steps, away from her. Away from the
temptation to let his selfish impulses rule. It would
be wrong to try to convince her they could have a
long and happy life together even without a child he'd
fathered. "You're young and beautiful and smart and
kind and a thousand other things I could mention.
Somewhere out there is a man who'll be able to give
you the gift of motherhood. It wouldn't be fair to you
to let things between us get serious."

Rachel rose slowly, a hand on the wall of the house
to steady herself as the swing wobbled behind her.
"Things were already getting serious."

Like he didn't know that.

"I can't pull you into a life that won't provide
something so important to you."

"Look…can't we think about this?" There was a

touch of desperation in her voice now. "I need some time to process everything. Please."

He ought to walk away—but how could he refuse those beseeching eyes? "I'll tell you what. Why don't we let things chill for a while and see how we both feel down the road?" That wasn't exactly a clean break, but it was the best he could do standing six feet away from her, cloaked in the scent of jasmine.

"How long is 'a while'?"

"Let's give ourselves a few weeks to settle back into our real lives at home." That should be long enough for her to realize her barely-there summertime romance wouldn't offer what she wanted out of life—and it would be easier to end things that way than with an abrupt break today. Even if that was the coward's way out.

Rachel's shoulders slumped. "When are you leaving?"

He wished he could say today. But he couldn't renege on his obligations here. "Gram's cast is supposed to come off next week. I'll be around until then."

"Maybe I'll see you before you go."

"It's a small island." Vague, but safe. In truth, he hoped they didn't meet again. The temptation to ditch his good intentions would be too strong.

She rubbed her palms down her shorts, then walked toward him. As she drew close, she reached for his hand and regarded him with those amazing jade eyes.

His lungs locked.

His fingers itched to stroke her cheek.

His arms longed to pull her close.

This wasn't good.

He needed to get out of there before he caved and claimed the kiss he'd been imagining for weeks.

"I want you to know that whatever happens, I'm glad our paths crossed." Her voice was shaky as she searched his eyes.

"Me, too."

A tear leaked out of her eye and trailed down her cheek.

Oh, man.

He might be a highly disciplined SEAL, but that single tear undid all his honorable intentions.

Maybe Rachel would never be his, but he wanted—needed—a memory to sustain him through all the dark days…and nights…to come.

Quashing the red alert pinging in his brain, Fletch lifted his unsteady hand and brushed back a wisp of soft hair that had come loose from her braid. When her breath hitched, when she began to tremble, his last smidgen of self-control shattered.

Cradling her face with his hands, he leaned down and captured her supple lips…hoping she'd give him one brief kiss, one sweet memory to carry in his heart.

She did more than that.

Moving into his arms, Rachel returned his kiss, holding nothing back, letting him know with every touch, every breath, every subtle shift in her position, how deep her feelings ran.

He wanted the kiss to last forever.

But nothing good did.

At last, digging deep for any dregs of the discipline he'd mastered as a SEAL, he broke contact.

Her respiration was as choppy as his as she clung to his arms.

"I need to go." His comment came out ragged.

Rachel didn't respond, only watched him through a shimmer of tears.

Swallowing, he eased back, turned away and strode to his SUV. Not until he was safely buckled into the passenger seat and rolling away did he dare look in his rearview mirror.

Rachel was still standing under the jasmine vine— and she remained there until he turned the corner and accelerated toward Gram's.

His one consolation was that she didn't want this to end any more than he did. He knew that as clearly as he knew he was doing the honorable thing.

Yet as far as he could see, it was over. He'd prayed last night for guidance and fortitude, and God had given him those. He'd found the strength to see this through, even if he'd died a little with every word.

As for his third request…he needed that more than ever.

Because only God's grace could ease the heaviness in his heart as he faced a future that didn't include Rachel.

Chapter Fourteen

"Well, that's good news." Aunt El entered the kitchen from the screen porch and slid the portable phone back into the holder on the counter.

"What?" Rachel turned from the sink. After a week with no Fletch, she could use a pick-me-up.

"Louise's cast came off today."

Rachel's spirits nosedived. That meant Louise's grandson was probably packing his bags at this very moment. He might even be planning to head home first thing in the morning.

Taking a glass from the cabinet, Eleanor studied her. "You don't look too happy about that."

"I'm happy for Louise." Rachel rinsed the silverware in her hand, doing her best to maintain a casual tone. "I suppose Fletch will be leaving soon."

"I believe she's convinced him to stay for the Francis House ribbon-cutting, when the Mitchell family arrives on Saturday. He worked hard on the project. He ought to be on hand for the payoff. The happy faces of our first guests should give everyone a boost."

"I suppose."

Aunt El snorted. "You sound about as enthusiastic as a patient preparing for a root canal." She filled the glass with water from the dispenser on the fridge, then faced her. "So are you ever going to tell me what happened between the two of you? Louise doesn't have a clue, and she says Fletch isn't talking, either."

After a full week to prepare for the inevitable questions, Rachel recited the answer she'd practiced. "He's a very nice man and we got along well, but we ran into a serious stumbling block."

"Serious for who?"

"Me." She had no doubt Fletch would advance full steam ahead if she gave him the green light. But hard as she'd tried, she couldn't manage to let go of her dream. She wanted to have more children someday. To shelter a tiny heart beside her own. To feel those magical movements of new life deep within her, knowing it was a life she and her husband had created in love.

"Does he have a secret wife hidden away somewhere?"

Rachel almost lost her grip on a drinking glass. "Of course not!"

The older woman took a sip of water and eyed

her. "I can't imagine anything else that would be insurmountable."

She might be able to if she knew the truth—but that was privileged information, and Rachel had no intention of betraying Fletch's confidence.

"Trust me, it's a huge hurdle."

"Hmm." Aunt El sat at the kitchen table and folded up their place mats from dinner. "It must be, if you're willing to pass up a chance for love with a hunky guy who has a whole lot to offer and is obviously smitten with you."

Rachel gripped a slippery plate in her hand and carefully fitted it into the dishwasher. "I know what I'm giving up, Aunt El."

"Do you?" Eleanor gathered a few crumbs on the table and made a neat little pile. "I wonder. As for obstacles—you know what they say. The only difference between stumbling blocks and stepping stones is the way you use them."

Drying her hands on the dish towel, Rachel leaned back against the counter. "Clever—but not always easy to implement."

"No one ever said the best things in life were easy." Eleanor stood and tucked the place mats into their drawer. "But they're worth fighting for—or waiting for—if you have the chance. And if love is deep and true, people manage to overcome their differences and make things work. They find a way to use obstacles to strengthen rather than destroy their relationship."

"That sounds nice in theory. But some problems aren't fixable."

Bandit trotted over to Eleanor, and she leaned down to give him a pat. "Everything is fixable except death—and with God's grace, even that can be a force for good, though it may take us a very long time to realize how." She smiled down at her canine companion. "What do you say we go watch the sunset and have a treat?"

The golden retriever's ears perked up and his tail began to swish in double-time as the duo started for the door.

Throat tightening, Rachel folded the dish towel into a neat square and wrapped her fingers around the edge of the counter. "I don't know how to fix this, Aunt El."

At her choked admission, the older woman turned back to her. "God does. If I were you, I'd ask for some advice before you let what could be the opportunity of a lifetime drive off into the sunset without you."

"I've already tried praying. I'm not getting any answers."

"Keep trying—and listening. Sometimes our answers come in unexpected ways."

"But Fletch is leaving in two days." A thread of desperation wove through her words.

"Putting God on a timetable, are we?" Aunt El sent her a pointed look. "Well, then, you best get at it."

With that, she and Bandit exited.

Through the sliding door, Rachel watched the two of them settle in on the porch, Aunt El in her favorite wicker chair, Bandit at her feet. The retriever waited patiently as she opened the box of dog biscuits she kept at hand.

Of course, it was easy to be patient when there was a guaranteed payoff.

Her prayers, on the other hand, had produced zilch.

She wandered over to the cabinet, selected a soothing peppermint brew, and went through the motions of making tea. Since her prayers weren't being answered, was it possible she'd been praying for the wrong thing? Maybe a generic request to fix the problem wasn't the best approach. Because, really, what was the problem? Fletch's medical issue? Based on what he'd said, that wasn't fixable, short of a miracle. And miracles like that were few and far between.

So what did she want God to fix? What would it take to give her story a happy ending?

The obvious answer was an attitude shift on her part. All she had to do was say it didn't matter if they never had children together.

Except it did.

She wanted children—and she wanted them to be

their biological offspring. It wasn't just about being pregnant. She could have a baby if she and Fletch got married. With modern medical procedures, women got pregnant every day without ever meeting the donor who'd made that gift possible.

But the whole clinical nature of that procedure turned her off. Besides, it wouldn't be Fletch's child. He or she wouldn't inherit his dark brown eyes or his strong jaw or his discipline or drive or integrity.

The microwave beeped and Rachel removed her tea, cradling the steaming mug in her hands as she trudged back to her room.

Okay, so her attitude wasn't PC. But it was honest. The clinical option that worked for a lot of women wasn't for her.

Which brought her right back to her starting place.

Leaving that method off the table, what else would give her a chance with Fletch and still allow her to be a mother?

Adoption was a possibility…but then their children wouldn't physically be part of *either* of them.

Sighing, she closed the door halfway behind her, propped some pillows against the headboard, and settled in. As tendrils of spicy peppermint steam rose toward her nose, she closed her eyes and once more turned to prayer.

God, I'm stuck. I was starting to believe Fletch was the answer to my prayer for a second chance at love and a family, but it seems he's the answer to only part of that prayer.

She took a sip of the soothing tea, letting the warmth chase away the chill that had lodged in her heart since the Fourth of July.

So am I being greedy? Should I be grateful for Fletch and forget about having any more babies? If that's what You want for me, how do I get to the place where I can honestly tell Fletch I've made peace with the situation? That I'll be content with...

A cold nose nudged her elbow, and she jerked, barely averting a peppermint geyser.

Bandit sat on his haunches beside the bed and offered her one of his goofy grins.

Shaking her head, Rachel reached over and patted him. "Did Aunt El send you in here to keep me company?"

Tongue lolling to one side, he tipped his head and emitted a yip.

"I'll take that as a yes. So what do you think I should do about this pickle I'm in, my friend? Let Fletch go, or grab hold and hang on tight?"

He inspected her for a moment, then gripped the blanket in his teeth and began tugging.

"Hey!" She balanced the tea in one hand and snatched a fistful of blanket with the other. "Let go! This isn't a game."

Shaking his head, he held on tighter.

She pulled harder.

Bandit gave a low growl deep in his throat and stared at her, as if to say, "Aren't you getting my message?"

Great.

Now she was looking to a dog for guidance.

"Okay, okay. I get your point. You think I should hang on tight. Now let go of the blanket." She gave another tug.

This time he released it. After trotting closer to lick her hand, he did a one-eighty and disappeared out the door.

Rachel sank back against her headboard and focused on the ceiling.

"Lord, I'm going to trust that wasn't Your answer to my plea for guidance, because I don't put a whole lot of credence in those kinds of signs. But if You could give me a message that's a little more definitive, I'd really appreciate it."

She finished off her tea and shimmied farther down into bed. It was too early to call it a night, but she wasn't up for another chat with Aunt El—or Bandit. Besides, given the insomnia that had plagued her since the Fourth of July, it couldn't hurt to try to catch up on a little shut-eye. Maybe the peppermint tea would soothe her into sleep. Perhaps the answer to her dilemma might even come to her in a dream.

At least that would be a bit more credible than a game of tug-of-war with a golden retriever.

* * *

Friday the thirteenth was living up to its name.

As Rachel juggled a box of books and groped for the door to the church office, the large manila envelope slid off the top and spiraled like a whirlybird to the ground, spewing Francis House receipts in all directions.

Dropping the box to the walkway with a thud, she dashed after the slips of paper scattering in the island breeze.

"Looks like you could use a hand."

Grabbing another receipt, she gave the clean-cut young man with the slightly kinky hair and latte-toned skin a quick once-over. He and an Asian girl who both appeared to be in their early twenties had joined in the chase.

"Thanks. I lost my grip on the box and things went downhill from there." Rachel kept moving, stuffing the receipts back into the envelope as she retrieved them.

With the three of them in pursuit, they managed to corral all the slips of paper in less than two minutes. After plucking the last one from the prickly clutches of a palmetto leaf, the young man handed it over to her.

"I think we got them all." He flashed her two rows of dazzling white teeth.

The Asian girl passed over her fistful of receipts, as well.

"Thank you both. I'd have been in deep doo doo with my aunt if I'd let any of those escape—and Reverend Carlson wouldn't be too happy, either."

The young man hoisted the box while the girl opened the door to the church office. "It's definitely smart to stay on the reverend's good side." He shot his companion a grin, which she returned.

So these two knew the minister. Interesting. She hadn't seen them at any of the Sunday services she'd attended.

He stepped aside, indicating Rachel should enter first, and she plunged into the welcome coolness, thanking him as she passed.

They followed her inside to the small, deserted office. A gone-to-lunch sign propped on the secretary's desk explained her absence, and Rachel sent an uncertain glance toward Reverend Carlson's closed door. She hated to bother the man. A note to the secretary about the receipts and the box of books from the attic room that Aunt El wanted to donate to the church's annual book fair should suffice.

The two young people, however, didn't seem to have any qualms about knocking on the minister's door. Or perhaps they had an appointment.

As she scanned the desk, searching for a blank sheet of paper, Reverend Carlson opened his door.

"Surprise!"

The two young people called out their greeting in unison, and Rachel turned toward the trio. An expression of pure joy spread over the minister's face, and he bear-hugged first one, then the other.

"Now, aren't you two a sight for sore eyes! I didn't think you were supposed to get here until tomorrow."

"We both managed to rearrange our schedules to eke out another day at home." The girl leaned close and nudged him with her shoulder. "Can you tell we missed you?"

"No more than I've missed you. Have you been to the house yet?"

"Yep." The young man grinned. "Mom sent us over to surprise you."

Rachel blinked.

Mom?

If the minister and his wife were the parents of these two young people, some serious adopting had gone on.

"She wants you to cut out early so we can go to Southern Soul for dinner and grab one of the indoor tables. It's too hot to sit outside." The girl linked her arm with his.

"Southern Soul—now that would be a treat." He patted her hand. "Your mom and I haven't been there since your last visit."

"You should go more often. St. Simons isn't that far."

"It's always more fun when you two tag along."

The young man draped his arm around the minister's shoulder. "Except for the time I dumped my fried okra in Esther's lap and she doused me with barbecue sauce in return."

The minister chuckled. "I must admit, that wasn't one of our most Norman-Rockwell-like moments. But it was memorable."

"So can you get away early, Dad?" The girl rose on tiptoe and kissed him on the cheek.

"To share some of Southern Soul's famous pulled pork and ribs with my favorite people in all the world? Count on it! Tell your mom I'll be home by three. And maybe after dinner we can stop at…" He caught sight of Rachel standing beside the secretary's desk. "My dear, I'm so sorry. I didn't even see you there in the midst of this family reunion."

She waved his apology aside. "No problem. I was just dropping off receipts for Francis House and some books for the book fair." She gestured to the box and the envelope. "I'll be out of your hair in a minute. I wouldn't want to delay that barbecue dinner you're planning."

"You won't, trust me. A visit from my children is always an incentive to play hooky." Reverend Carlson flashed them both a grin, then drew them toward her. "Let me introduce you to the smartest CPA in Atlanta and a future Pulitzer-Prize-winning reporter—who also happen to be my daughter and son. Rachel, meet Esther and M.J.—short for Moses James."

After they all shook hands and exchanged a few

pleasantries, the two young people left with a reminder to the minister to come home as soon as possible.

He waved them off from the front door and turned to Rachel. "Sorry for the bragging. If I sound like a proud dad, that's because I am."

"They seem like very nice young people."

"Indeed they are. And they've been a great blessing in our lives. One we never expected to have."

His comment invited further conversation, so Rachel dipped a toe in. "I assume they're adopted."

"An astute observation." The minister's eyes twinkled. "Let me tell you, we drew some strange looks in public when the children were small, what with Susan's blond hair and my fair Swedish skin. We were quite the motley crew."

"As far as I can see, those looks didn't have any negative impact on your children. They strike me as very well-adjusted young adults."

"They are. But when I think where those two might have ended up..." He shook his head. "Fortunately, their stories had a happy ending—as did Susan's and mine."

Rachel bit her lip. The man had places to go. She shouldn't delay him. Yet in light of his experience with adoption, might he have some insights that would help her as she struggled with her own dilemma?

"My intuition tells me you have some questions."

She conceded his observation with a shrug, choosing her words with care. "The concept of adoption interests me. I'm curious about why people make that choice."

"I've had a lot practice talking about that over the years while counseling potential adoptive parents—particularly those who are considering adopting children of other races. If you'd like to come into my office for a few minutes, I'd be happy to answer any questions you have."

"I don't want to delay your dinner."

"You won't. I can wrap up the most critical things on my to-do list in another twenty minutes if I push myself—and my children just gave me a great incentive to do that. The rest can wait until Monday."

"All right. Thank you."

Reverend Carlson followed her into the office and gestured to a grouping of comfortable chairs in one corner. "Let's sit there. It's more conducive to conversation."

While she settled into one of the plush seats, his phone rang and he gave her an apologetic look. "Do you mind if I take that? The air conditioner in the church is giving us fits, and I've been expecting to hear from the repairman. I'd like to get him out here today or we'll *all* be in the hot seat on Sunday."

"By all means. Take your time."

As Reverend Carlson moved behind his desk and began to converse with the man, Rachel examined the unpretentious office. The desk was piled high with books. Several were open, and a long page of handwritten notes was front and center, as if he'd been working on Sunday's sermon. Family pictures shared space with yet more books on the large shelving unit against one wall. She had no trouble recognizing Esther and M.J. in a series of shots that marked the passage of years. The walls contained more photos, along with some framed scripture passages.

She leaned closer to read the latter, which were done in calligraphy and grouped together on the wall in front of her. The quotes were from a variety of books, and all were themed around adoption.

"Those are particular favorites of mine." The minister rejoined her, pointing to two adjacent passages.

She read them again, first the one from Psalms, then the one from Hosea.

"Even if my father and mother forsake me, the Lord will take me in."

"For in you the orphan finds compassion."

"I've amassed quite a collection over the years." Reverend Carlson settled into a chair beside her.

"So you've always been interested in adoption."

"No. At least, not in a personal sense. Susan and I always hoped to have a family of our own, but after she had a series of progressively more serious miscarriages, it became clear that route was too dangerous. Adoption wasn't on our radar in the beginning, though. I suppose we were so disappointed by our failure to become biological parents that we were blind to other possibilities. And back in those sad days, the notion of raising someone else's child didn't hold a whole lot appeal."

Rachel leaned forward and knotted her hands in her lap. This didn't quite match her own situation, but it was close. "What happened to change your mind?"

"Not what, but who. One cold winter morning, a few years into my ministry, I found a homeless seventeen-year-old sleeping in a pew in my first church. She'd come to the Sunday service, hidden in the ladies room and spent the night. After Susan and I fed her, she told us she was pregnant—and teetering on the verge of abortion. Between the two of us, we convinced her to give the decision more thought. I hooked her up with an excellent counseling agency, and she decided to carry the baby to term and put it up for adoption. She and I had many conversations during those months, and in the end she asked if Susan and I would consider adopting her child. That was M.J.'s mother."

"Wow." Rachel let out a slow breath. "That was a lot for her to ask of you—and a lot for you to take on."

"Susan and I would have agreed with you before we met M.J.'s mother. But over the months we knew her, we both concluded God had brought her into our lives to offer us another chance to be parents. All we had to do was trust in Him and follow the path He was laying out for us."

"You make that sound easy."

"Far from it. We knew raising a biracial baby would bring many challenges—but we felt confident love would conquer those. So by the time M.J.'s mother approached us, we were considering the very thing she asked."

"What about Esther?"

"She came to us two years later. Susan and I were on a mission trip to Korea, and as part of our visit we did some volunteer work at an orphanage. Esther was two and a half, and from the moment she and Susan laid eyes on each other it was love at first sight. I wasn't far behind. Since everything had worked out beautifully with M.J., giving him a sister seemed the most natural thing in the world. We set the process in motion even before we left the country."

Rachel tried to think of a delicate way to phrase her next question. "So did you ever feel any regret or…" she tried to find the right words, "as if you'd missed something beautiful by not having your own biological children?"

Reverend Carlson rested his elbows on the arms of his chair, linked his fingers and leaned back. "In the beginning, after we realized that wasn't an option for us, we both went through a grieving process. It's hard to let go of a dream. Yet clinging to one dream can blind you to the possibility of other, perhaps better, dreams. Meeting M.J.'s mother helped us see that."

"And your wife felt the same?"

"It was harder for her. Susan had always wanted to have a baby…or two or three. But I'll never forget what she said to me one night as she was rocking M.J., not long after we brought him home from the hospital. Her words are still as clear to me as if she spoke them yesterday." His gaze strayed toward the family photo on the small table between them.

Rachel leaned forward again.

"She said, 'You know, a woman only carries a baby inside her for nine months—a very small part of both their lives. Maybe M.J. doesn't have my blond hair or your blue eyes, but we're going to give him something even more important that's as much a part of us as our physical features—our values and principles and faith. If we do our job well, he's going to carry that part of us with him his whole life.'"

Reverend Carlson smiled, his features placid, his expression content. "She was right, as usual. We might have missed out on one beautiful experience, but this one has been just as beautiful…and we'd have missed *it* if we'd had biological children. Life is about trade-offs, and sometimes what you get is far better than what you give up."

Silence fell in the room while Rachel processed all the minister had said.

And as the seconds ticked by, her concerns suddenly seemed petty. Yes, she'd enjoyed being pregnant—but was holding out for that experience worth the loss of Fletch? And Susan had a valid point: shared eye or hair color was trivial in comparison to the more important things a parent could pass on to a child, especially one in desperate need of loving. There would be a trade-off, but perhaps it would be a positive one.

"Have I answered all your questions, Rachel?"

At the minister's gentle question, she refocused on him. "Yes. And you've given me a lot to think about."

"Adoption is a wonderful thing, whatever the impetus for choosing it. After all, God adopted each of us. Remember what Paul wrote in Galatians, 'But when the fullness of time had come, God sent His Son, born of a woman, born under the law, to ransom those under the law, so that we might receive adoption.' It seems somehow fitting to pass that gift of adoption on to children who are in need, don't you think?"

"Yes. And it's obvious that decision has brought you and your wife great happiness. I appreciate your willingness to share your story." Rachel checked her watch and stood. "I'm sorry I delayed you this long. Please apologize for me to your family for bending your ear."

Reverend Carlson rose, too, and followed her to the door. "God's work always comes first. They all understand that. And I have a feeling I was doing His work just now."

At the threshold, Rachel paused. "You were. I've been praying for guidance about a certain issue, and I think our conversation was the answer to that prayer."

"Then it was time well spent. Tell Eleanor I'll get those invoices taken care of, and please thank her for the books."

"I will. Enjoy your evening with your family."

Rachel crossed the still-empty outer office. Strange how things worked. If the secretary had been here, she might not have stayed long enough to witness the exchange between the minister and his children. It was odd, too, that the two young people happened to arrive while she was chasing receipts.

She pushed through the outside door. Aunt El had said the answer to prayers often came in unexpected ways, and the past twenty minutes seemed to validate that.

Yet her conversation with the pastor raised other questions.

Could she apply his experience to her own situation?

Could she root out the selfishness in her heart and take a path different from the one she'd planned?

Could she find as much joy in adoption as she would in having a biological child of her own?

And could she answer all those questions before Fletch left for Norfolk in less than twenty-four hours?

The last question was critical.

Because even though he'd suggested they allow things to chill for a while, she had a sinking feeling that if she let him leave the island with the situation unresolved, their relationship was over. A decisive man like Fletch would interpret her waffling as uncertainty, and he'd already made it clear he didn't want her to make compromises she might later regret. This wasn't about making a choice she could merely live with; it was about making a choice she could embrace with joy.

At some instinctive level, Rachel knew Fletch expected her to choose the possibility of love and biological children with some future suitor over the reality of the love he was ready to offer her now.

A week ago, he might have been right.

But after a lot of prayer and some serious enlightenment, she was fast coming to a different conclusion.

A family with Fletch—no matter how that family was created—was far preferable to a family with any other potential husband she might meet. Her former Navy SEAL was the kind of man who came along for most women once in a lifetime…if they were lucky. And she'd already been twice blessed on that score. She should be grateful, not greedy.

So for the rest of today she'd think about everything Reverend Carlson had said. She'd also take a long walk on the beach and do some serious praying.

But unless some dramatic development changed her mind, come tomorrow she was going to look Fletch in the eye and make sure he knew that choosing him wasn't a compromise.

It was a blessing.

Chapter Fifteen

❧

"A packed suitcase at the end of a visit is one of the saddest sights in the world."

At the comment, Fletch turned toward the door of the guest bedroom. Arms folded, expression glum, Gram was surveying his bags, lined up with military precision on the floor in front of the dresser.

"I'll be back for Thanksgiving."

"That's four months away."

He crossed the room and gave her a hug. "I'll call you often, I promise."

She squeezed him back, her spiky hair tickling his nose. Funny how he'd grown to like her new look—and spunky new attitude—over the past few weeks.

When Gram drew back, she lifted her chin and touched his cheek. "I wish I could put a smile back on that face. Would it help if I modeled my bird-of-paradise muumuu for you? You got a hearty laugh the first time you saw it."

His lips twitched at the thought of the gaudy garment. "I'm not sure my eyes could take a second hit."

She gave him a playful nudge with her shoulder. "I'll have you know I ordered that direct from Hawaii."

"I believe it. Now you just need to learn how to do the hula."

That earned him a finger poke in the chest. "Don't you make fun of me, young man. Now that this—" she waved her cast-free wrist "—is healed, I might take you up on that challenge."

Gram doing the hula.

A chuckle rumbled in his chest.

"There now, that's better." She gave him a pleased look. "You're so much more handsome with a smile instead of that fierce scowl you've been wearing for the past week."

The corners of his mouth flattened, and he turned away on the pretext of retrieving his cell.

Gram followed him, tucking her arm in his as he slid the phone into his belt. "I'm sorry things didn't work out with Rachel. I don't know what happened, and I'm not asking you to tell me, but it's such a shame. I had high hopes for the two of you."

"You've been reading too many of those romance novels you like. Real life doesn't always have happy endings."

"Sometimes it does."

"Not this time."

"I suppose not." She sighed. "We have two hours before the ribbon cutting. Could I commandeer you once more for chauffeur duty? I'd like to run by Francis House and put the carrot cake for the Mitchells in the fridge. If I take it to the festivities at noon, it won't be a surprise. I'd drive myself, but this wrist is a lot weaker than I expected, and I'd rather not be trying to turn the wheel on the car until I have a few more physical-therapy sessions under my belt."

"Sure. You want to do it now?" At least running an errand would give him something to do besides sit around lamenting about what might have been with Rachel.

"Now is perfect. And let's take my car. It's been sitting in the garage so long I want to make certain it still runs."

"Not a bad idea."

Less than ten minutes later, Fletch swung Gram's sporty red Camaro into the driveway of the house where he'd spent some of his happiest hours on the island—thanks to Rachel.

Suppressing the familiar surge of regret, he set the brake and gestured to the dessert Gram was cradling in her lap. "The Mitchells are in for a treat. No one bakes a better carrot cake than you."

Gram waved off the praise but looked pleased nonetheless. "You're prejudiced."

"The judges in that bake-off you entered a few years ago in Nashville weren't."

Spots of color appeared in her cheeks. "I'm sure there were many other fine entries. They just must have been in the mood for carrot cake that day." Before he could disagree, she gestured to the house. "No sense both of us trekking inside. Would you mind putting this in the fridge? Eleanor gave me a key the other day when we were running back and forth adding all the finishing touches."

"Sure." Fletch started to turn off the car, but she stopped him with a hand on his arm. "Leave it on, please. The day's warming up, and the cool air feels nice."

"Not a bad idea. Sit tight and I'll come around for the cake."

Sixty seconds later, cake in hand, Fletch took the pewter keychain she held out.

"Nice touch, don't you think?" Gram gestured to the image of Francis of Assisi molded into the metal.

"Yeah. You and the crew thought of everything." He stepped back and grasped the edge of the door. "I'll be back in a minute."

Gram leaned forward and flipped on the radio. "Don't rush. My favorite talk show is on."

As she folded her hands in her lap and settled back in her seat, Fletch closed the door and walked toward the front door. The sweet scent of jasmine invaded his nostrils as he passed underneath the arbor, and he picked up his pace, sparing a quick glance at the swing he and Rachel had shared the night his dreams had crumbled.

If only things could have been different.

If only he could be less noble.

If only her feelings for him had been strong enough to compensate for the sacrifice that loving him would require.

But it was a waste of time to wish for what couldn't be.

Clamping his lips together, he juggled the cake in one hand and fitted the key in the lock with the other.

As the door swung open, he looked back at Gram. Her head was turned his direction, and she lifted her hand and wiggled her fingers. Then she used both hands to pull up the corners of her mouth.

He tried to coax his own lips to respond, but they wouldn't budge.

Once in the tiny foyer, he closed the door to keep the hot air outside and headed toward the refrigerator, letting his gaze roam over the living room, dining area and kitchen. Rachel's and his handiwork was evident in the pristine moldings and the long, inviting swaths of cream-colored paint on the walls.

No question about it, the remodeling project had worked wonders, transforming the dingy dwelling into a welcoming, light-filled haven. If his own visit to Jekyll Island was ending on a gloomy note, at least he'd participated in an endeavor that would bring joy to countless families for years to come.

In the kitchen, he opened the fridge—only to discover that other members of Gram's congregation must have had the same idea. The shelves were stocked with cold cuts, fresh fruit, a foil-covered casserole with baking instructions taped to the top, milk, eggs, orange juice…and a bunch of other stuff.

Throttling a groan, Fletch tossed the key on the counter and set about rearranging the contents. All he needed was enough space to wedge in the cake. Considering how tightly he'd once packed his SEAL gear, this ought to be a cinch.

Three minutes later, after shuffling the contents twice, he finally managed to squeeze in the cake with a quarter inch to spare.

Key once more in hand, he retraced his steps toward the front door, detouring to take one last look at the whimsical dolphin mural Rachel had painted.

He stood for a moment on the threshold as he took in all the clever details designed to delight the children who would occupy this room: the baby dolphin she'd added in the background since his last visit; the sailor-hat-wearing pelican, swooping low to take a gander at the game of beach ball; the candy-cane-striped lighthouse in the background with a giant Hersey Kiss instead of a lantern room at the top.

The youngsters who inhabited this room were going to love it.

All the playful, kid-pleasing touches were yet

another reminder that Rachel was meant to be a mother—and that she should marry a man who could give her the chance to have that total experience.

Fletch sucked in a sharp breath.

It was time to leave.

Turning, he strode down the short hall, opened the front door, took one step out—and froze.

Two things had changed since he'd entered.

Gram's car was gone from the driveway.

And Rachel was sitting on the top step, under the arching jasmine vine.

"Hi." She gave him a tentative smile.

Fletch scanned the empty driveway again and frowned. "What's going on?"

"I thought I'd stop by the house before the crowd arrived."

He narrowed his eyes, adding things up. "Was this a setup?"

Rachel twirled a sprig of jasmine in her fingers. "If you're asking me whether I knew exactly how this scene was going to play out, the answer is no. But Louise did agree to get you here at ten o'clock."

As she paraphrased the reply he'd given to that same question on the Fourth of July, he tried to rein in the little surge of hope that ticked up his pulse.

"That sounds familiar."

She lifted the jasmine to her nose, her gaze locked

on his. "It should. You gave me a similar response when you were looking to share some fireworks."

Fletch moved a step closer. "So what's your excuse?"

"I had fireworks in mind, too."

He swallowed. "The holiday's over."

"I'd like to think *our* celebration is just beginning."

The hope he was trying to restrain began to percolate. "I thought we were going to give each other some space."

"No. You were going to give *me* some space. I don't need it anymore." Rachel patted the step beside her. "Want to join me?"

Was she kidding?

In silence, he crossed the porch, settled down beside her—and waited.

"I've been doing a lot of thinking…and praying… during the past week." She set the jasmine beside her and clasped her hands around her knees, giving him her full attention. "And if you still want to see where things between us might lead, I'm ready…and willing…to sign on for that mission."

His pulse thundering in his ears, Fletch tried to corral the thoughts pinging through his brain. Could this be for real, when less than ten minutes ago he'd been berating himself about wishing for things he couldn't have?

But Rachel looked real enough, sitting inches away in a curve-hugging green knit top and khaki shorts, the gentle breeze toying with the soft wisps of hair that had escaped her braid.

In the lengthening silence, a shadow of uncertainty darkened her irises to a dusky jade, and the edges of her mouth quivered. "That is, unless you've changed your mind?"

"No." His answer came out fast and sure. "But why did you change yours?"

"I had an illuminating experience. Would you like to hear about it?"

"Yeah. I would."

He listened as she told him of her encounter with the minister's adopted children and her subsequent conversation with Reverend Carlson.

As the story wound down, she reached over and placed her hand on his knee. Even through the fabric of his jeans he could feel the warmth of her fingers. "Here's the thing, Fletch. After Mark died, I never expected to love again. Only in the past couple of months have I begun to allow for the possibility that somewhere far down the road it might happen—and I assumed children would go along with that. You definitely weren't on my agenda for this summer. But God's timing isn't always ours…nor do his plans always mesh with ours."

Fletch scrutinized her, wanting to believe she was at peace with the fact that a union with him wouldn't produce any biological offspring. That adoption was truly an option she could embrace. That her feelings for him—and the electricity that buzzed in the air whenever they were together—weren't clouding her thinking and leading her to make a choice she'd later regret.

She spoke as if she'd read his mind. "In case you're concerned, despite the fact there's enough voltage zipping between us to light up the state of Georgia, my judgment hasn't been compromised by overactive hormones."

"That's good to know. And I like everything you said." Fletch spoke slowly, struggling to rein in the burgeoning euphoria that was short-circuiting the left side of his brain. "But you made this decision pretty fast."

Rachel tipped her head, her expression pensive. "The odd thing is, it doesn't feel fast at all. To be honest, the past week has seemed like an eternity. And every day that went by without seeing you moved me further along the path toward this decision. But after yesterday's experience at church, it was like a light was flipped on. All at once, I could see things clearly—and I knew with absolute certainty that choosing you wasn't a compromise. It was a blessing."

As Fletch looked down into the eyes that had haunted his dreams for the past week, pressure built in his throat. There was no deceit or uncertainty in their depth, only conviction and peace and hope.

Most of all, hope.

The same hope that was bubbling up and spilling over in his heart.

Fletch wove his fingers through hers. "No one's ever called me a blessing before. In fact, Gram had a few other choice words for me after Fourth of July."

"Believe me, I got my share of those, too, from Aunt El. Well deserved, I might add. But if this is heading where I think it is, I expect we'll soon be redeemed."

"All must be forgiven already if they helped plan this little rendezvous."

"Oh, they were both eager to cooperate."

"I'll bet."

"So are we good?" Rachel searched his face, a hint of anxiety creeping into her voice.

"We're good. As a matter of fact, I think we're going to be very good." He gave her a slow, intimate smile that brought a flush to her cheeks. "However…I still want to take things slow. We haven't known each other that long. You could have second thoughts."

"Not a chance."

At the conviction in her tone, his smile broadened. "I like a woman who knows her mind. But we're going to play this safe. I don't want any regrets down the road."

Rachel made a face. "I thought Navy SEALs were men of action who charged into the thick of things."

"Only after careful planning and reconnaissance. At the moment, we're in the reconnaissance phase."

"Hmm." She picked up the sprig of jasmine and studied it. "That's going to be a bit of a challenge. The logistics will be a hassle once we're both back on our home turf."

"We only live a hundred miles apart, according to MapQuest. Besides, SEALs are experts at logistics."

Rachel scooted closer, until her leg was brushing his, and proceeded to play with a button on his shirt. "What other expertise do you claim?"

At her flirty inflection, Fletch grabbed her hand, tugged her to her feet and urged her up onto the porch.

"Hey! Where are we going?"

"Away from prying eyes. Any complaints?"

She didn't say a word.

Once hidden behind the dense jasmine vine, he swung around and pulled her into his arms. "Now... to answer your question about SEAL expertise, we're also rumored to have a way with the ladies."

Grinning, Rachel lifted her arms and linked them around his neck. "Want to demonstrate that?"

As his eyes began to smolder, he gave her a slow, toe-curling smile. "My very next mission."

And in the perfumed air of the jasmine vine, on the porch of the haven they'd helped create, under the sunny skies of their special Golden Isle, he did.

Epilogue

Four months later

Could a Thanksgiving be more perfect?

Rachel lifted her face to the sun and drew in a lungful of the tangy salt air. It might not be close to the record high temperature for November 22 on Jekyll Island, but she'd take seventy-two degrees and blue skies any day.

Still, the great weather paled in comparison to the amazing man at her side, his hand firmly linked with hers as they crossed the dune bridge to the beach.

She looked at him—only to find him gazing at her.

"I'm thinking the same thing." The warmth in his eyes added a few degrees to the balmy temperature. "It's a perfect holiday."

She squeezed his hand as they started down the steps to the sand. "It's nice to be back, isn't it?"

"Yeah. Commuting between Gram's house and

Eleanor's is a whole lot easier than the drive from Norfolk to Richmond."

"I warned you the distance would be a problem."

"Frustrating is a better word. Every time I make the drive, I keep wishing I could be sharing those hours with you instead of listening to talk radio."

"Hopefully, the distance won't be an issue forever."

Despite the broad hint, Fletch didn't respond as they stepped onto the sand.

Rachel stifled her disappointment. At this point, she was more than ready to take things to the next level. Truth be told, she'd been ready for weeks. Yet hard as she'd tried to convey that in every possible way, Fletch's resolve hadn't wavered. He wanted to give her a chance to second-guess her decision.

Except she never had. If anything, she was more certain than ever that loving the man at her side was right and good and part of God's plan for her.

There'd been one positive outcome from their months apart, however. She'd had plenty of time to do lots of research on adoption. That, too, felt right and good and part of God's plan. There were so many children in need of loving homes. Together she and Fletch could offer a few of them a chance they might not otherwise have. They'd still be creating a child together…but in a different way, just as Reverend Carlson and his wife had.

Maybe one of these days she'd convince him she

wasn't only ready but eager to take the next step in their relationship and make a serious commitment.

But today she was going to push those thoughts aside and enjoy the holiday with him on their beloved island.

Rachel leaned down to pet the golden retriever who was trotting along beside them on the deserted beach. "Do you think Aunt El and Louise bought our excuse about wanting to give Bandit a chance to stretch his legs?"

"Are you kidding? It was an obvious ruse to give us some time alone together. They're probably back at your aunt's, chattering away about us while they fuss over the turkey."

"I thought the Frisbee added some legitimacy." Rachel waved the blue disk in her hand.

"Not much—but it was a nice touch." Fletch took it from her, examining the faint teeth marks on the edge. "Is this the infamous Frisbee Bandit mistook for my swim fin?"

"The very same."

He gave it a toss, toward the spot where he'd been standing the day they'd met. Bandit took off after it, legs churning the sand.

"I remember how horrified I was when he barreled straight for you." Rachel couldn't help cringing as Bandit leaped in the air and snatched the Frisbee, a replay of their first disastrous encounter running through her mind.

"And I remember how you made it very clear he wasn't your dog—after you stared at my leg."

She gave him a cheeky grin. "I still stare at your legs—for a different reason now."

One side of his mouth hitched up. "I think that's supposed to be a guy's line."

"Too late. I stole it."

"So is that some kind of come-on?" Fletch took the Frisbee from Bandit after the dog skidded to a stop beside him.

"Why ever would you think that?" Rachel batted her eyelashes at him.

Fletch gave that slow, deep chuckle she loved, then examined the Frisbee. "You know, I think we should preserve this. Maybe even frame it. It's the stuff of family legend. Someday our grandchildren would probably get a big kick out of the story behind it."

Rachel gaped at him.

Grandchildren?

This from the man who'd set the snail pace in their relationship? Who redirected conversations whenever they veered too close to topics like this?

Slowly Fletch reached into the pocket of his jeans and withdrew a small, velvet jewelry box.

Her heart stumbled.

"I intended to wait until Christmas for this, but I have to confess my patience wore thin. However, if you want me to keep it for another month, I can do that."

"No!" Her response came out in a squeak, and she cleared her throat. "My patience is on its last legs, too."

"I don't want to rush you, Rachel." His tone grew more serious. "I want you to be sure."

"I was sure four months ago."

He searched her eyes, and his own warmed. Then he flipped up the lid to display a stunning marquise-shaped diamond flanked by three smaller diamonds on each side.

"Wow." Rachel stared at the ring, the facets of the stones sparkling in the island sun.

"Does that mean it meets with your approval?"

"That would be a safe conclusion."

A quiver ran through the fingers of the steadiest man she knew as he removed the ring. After slipping the box back into his pocket, he took her hand. "I've been waiting all my life for this day."

At his husky words, pressure built in her throat. "We only met in July."

"I know. But I always believed there was a woman for me out there somewhere, and that in God's time I'd meet her, we'd fall in love, marry and raise a family. It was supposed to be simple and straight-forward—until Afghanistan complicated things."

A flicker of distress tightened his features, and Rachel lifted her hand to smooth the creases from his brow. "We can make things simple again, Fletch.

Because in the end, love is all that matters. And I love you with all my heart."

He gave her an amused look. "You stole my line again."

"You can say it, too."

"I will." He lowered himself to one knee—only to have Bandit nose in, hoping for more fun and games. Fletch eased him back with a gentle but firm hand. "Go chase the sand crabs, Bandit. I have some important business to take care of here."

Head drooping, the retriever skulked a few feet away and plopped down on the sand, regarding them with a doleful expression.

Fletch looked up at her, and the love shining in his eyes took her breath away even before he spoke the words. "The truth is, you're the woman I've been waiting for, Rachel. You're loving and kind and smart and compassionate and giving and fun to be with—the whole package, beautiful inside and out. I love you more than I thought I could ever love anyone, and I can't imagine spending the rest of my life without you. So," he lifted her hand, "would you…"

Once more, Bandit nosed in to sniff at the ring poised over Rachel's finger.

"Oh, for heaven's sake!" Rachel sent her aunt's dog an exasperated scowl. "Go away, Bandit!" She flung the Frisbee as hard as she could, and as he took off running she redirected her attention to the man on one knee in front of her. "If I'd known this was in your plans for the day, I'd never have brought him."

Fletch, good sport that he was, just grinned. "Another story to tell our grandchildren. Where were we?"

"Here." She wiggled her finger.

"Right." Once more he positioned the ring. His Adam's apple bobbed, and he took a deep breath. "Rachel Shaw, will you do me the honor of becoming my wife?"

Above the crash of the surf and the caw of the gulls, she was certain she heard violins.

"Yes." Though the word came out breathless, it rang with conviction.

Fletch slid the ring onto her finger, started to rise—and then pitched toward her as a mass of golden fur bumped him from behind.

The next thing Rachel knew, she was lying in the sand, tangled in Fletch's arms. Beside them, Bandit dropped the Frisbee on the beach.

"This is so not how I expected your proposal to go, whenever it came." Despite herself, Rachel couldn't quash the chuckle bubbling up inside.

Fletch rolled over and propped himself up one elbow next to her. "You're not hurt, are you?"

"Nope." She twisted her head and looked at his strong, handsome face, framed against the cloudless blue sky.

"I'm sorry about that. It's not the way I expected things to go, either."

"The outcome's the same, though." She lifted her hand and wiggled her finger. "And lying on the sand with a handsome SEAL isn't such a bad end to a proposal. It's kind of like that beach scene in *From Here to Eternity.*"

"You think?"

"Yeah. I think." Out of the corner of her eye she caught Bandit creeping close again.

"As for you…" Rachel gave him a stern frown. "Go. Away. Now. Sit. Stay."

Apparently her no-nonsense tone convinced the retriever there would be no more frivolities—for him. Heaving what sounded like a disgruntled snuffle, he marched off, turned and stretched out to catch some rays, facing away from them.

Rachel smiled back at Fletch. "You're on. Let's seal this engagement with a proper kiss."

He leaned over and traced her lips with a fingertip, sending a delicious shiver up her spine. "You know, Gram and Aunt El could very well be up in the sky room watching us."

"That thought did occur to me. So why don't we give them something to watch, since they instigated this whole thing?"

Fletch moved in close, until his lips were a whisper away and his breath was warm on her cheek. "I like how you think."

Smiling, Rachel put her arms around his neck and tugged. "Prove it."

And as the palms trees swayed above them, he did just that.

* * * * *

Dear Reader,

Welcome to Jekyll Island, a beautiful barrier island off the coast of Georgia that holds many happy memories for me.

As I prepared to write this book, I traveled back to this special place, wanting to refresh my memories—and hoping it was the way I remembered it. I'm happy to say, in a very positive way, that this Golden Isle still remains largely untouched by the outside world.

In *Second Chance Summer,* Rachel and Fletch come to the island for reasons that have nothing to do with romance. But God has other plans in mind for them—plans that don't necessarily fit with their own. And isn't that how it often is? God throws us a curveball that ends up leading to a home run.

I hope you enjoy your visit to my magical island—and reading about this special couple—as much as I enjoyed writing the story.

Please check my website at www.irenehannon.com for more information about my other books, or follow me on Facebook. And do join me for another captivating romance or romantic suspense novel soon!

Irene Hannon

Questions for Discussion

1. What was your favorite moment in the opening scene? Why? Have you ever met someone under less-than-ideal circumstances? How did that color your impression of the person going forward?

2. Madeleine's story seems to have a happy ending, but do you know any children like her, whose parents are too busy with their own lives and careers to give enough time to their offspring? How might that affect the child in the future?

3. How did you feel about Madeleine's mother initially? Did your feelings change after you learned about her background? Why or why not?

4. Losing a leg—or coping with any disability—is a huge challenge. Why was Fletch able to overcome his impediment and lead a normal life?

5. In light of the couple's respective tragedies, why do you think Rachel's faith remained strong and Fletch's faltered? How would you counsel someone who is going through a tough time and whose faith is eroding?

6. In the end, Rachel gives up her dream of carrying a child. Do you think she will ever regret this? Why or why not? Support your answer with examples from the book.

7. The island church's Francis House project was designed to help deserving families who wouldn't otherwise be able to afford a vacation. Have you ever been involved in a project that you believed was a living testament to your faith?

8. Lisa, the wife of Fletch's SEAL partner, has decided her husband would want her to live fully rather than mourn his death forever. Based on what she told Fletch, do you think she was right? Why do people often feel guilt about moving on after the loss of a loved one?

9. Fletch was faced with a horrendous decision in Afghanistan—kill people who were possibly innocent or risk being killed. How would you feel if you were in that situation? What long-term repercussions might that kind of pressure have on a person's life?

10. The author says in her dedication and letter that Jekyll Island holds a special place in her heart. Do you have a place like that? Where is it, and what makes it so special?

11. Eleanor and Louise are well into their senior years when they meet and strike up a friendship. At one point, Louise says, "Funny how you can go through your whole life and then, in the last stages, find the best friend you ever had." Have you had different best friends throughout your life? Why do you think friendships change? Do you have a friend you've known your whole life?

12. The jasmine vine appears in several memorable scenes, and that scent will be indelibly etched in Rachel's and Fletch's memories. Is there any scent that brings back memories for you? Talk about that.

13. What is the one thing you will most remember about this book? Why?

LARGER-PRINT BOOKS!

GET 2 FREE
LARGER-PRINT NOVELS
PLUS 2 FREE
MYSTERY GIFTS

Love Inspired®

SUSPENSE
RIVETING INSPIRATIONAL ROMANCE

Larger-print novels are now available...

LISLPDIR13R